NIGHT STALKER

Simon halted. His bluff hadn't worked. The flickering torchlight suggested the creature crouched low to the ground, poised to pounce. He still could not tell what animal they were dealing with.

"Simon?" Felicity said uncertainly. She had moved between the thing and their son so that to get at Peter it had to go through her. "Back away. Come over here with us."

Good advice, Simon thought. But to his horror, each time he took a step back, the thing took a step forward. He stopped after three steps, unwilling to draw it closer. But the thing did not stop. It kept slinking toward him.

The eastern sky had been brightening the whole while. Between the harbinger of dawn and Simon's brand, he finally saw the creature clearly enough to identify it. "No!" he breathed.

It was a wolf.

A huge timber wolf.

The *Wilderness* series:

WILDERNESS #53:
THE RISING STORM

DAVID THOMPSON

LEISURE BOOKS NEW YORK CITY

Dedicated to Judy, Shane, Joshua, and Kyndra.

A LEISURE BOOK®

September 2007

Published by

Dorchester Publishing Co., Inc.
200 Madison Avenue
New York, NY 10016

ISBN-10: 0-8439-5929-0
ISBN-13: 978-0-8439-5929-1

Printed in the United States of America.

Visit us on the web at www.dorchesterpub.com.

WILDERNESS #53:
THE RISING STORM

Chapter One

The Garden of Eden had its serpent.

Which is why it was fitting that Simon and Felicity Ward named the valley where they had settled after the first of all gardens. Situated amid emerald foothills that bordered the towering Rocky Mountains, the valley was their notion of paradise on earth.

Thanks to a year-round stream fed by runoff from the snow that crowned the highest peaks, Simon and Felicity had done a wondrous thing. They were the first homesteaders to have a thriving farm. Seeds they brought from Boston were the key to their success. Seeds for corn, wheat, barley, tomatoes, potatoes, lettuce and more. The Wards planted those seeds and nurtured the resultant seedlings and reaped a bountiful harvest.

All was not perfect, though. The growing season was not as long as Simon liked. Spring did not come until late, and fall came much too early, but with careful planning the Wards had accomplished what many claimed was impossible. They were wresting a living from the wilds.

Their homestead was a model of efficiency. Their farm was the talk of the territory. It was talked about at Bent's Fort, where trappers and mountain men and Indians and settlers came to trade and obtain supplies and socialize.

The two strangers who stayed at the trading post for a week heard about the Ward farm. Indeed, when the Wards and their valley were first mentioned by the blacksmith in casual conversation, the pair could not hear enough. They plied the blacksmith and everyone else at Bent's Fort with questions about the Wards and their achievements, but they did so in such a way that no one realized how intensely interested they were.

The strangers were from England. One was named Severn, the other York. Severn did most of the asking. He was tall and broad of shoulder, with a severe face and a long nose that he looked down when he talked to people. He had an air about him that some of the mountain men disliked, but since he was free with his money and bought drinks for everyone he talked to—a lot of drinks if they knew a lot about the Wards and their valley—his arrogant manner was overlooked.

Severn claimed he and York were looking for a site to homestead. After a week the pair left, and no one gave them any thought. No one wondered why they often huddled together and whispered and then became quiet if others strayed near. No one thought much of the fact that for homesteaders, they did not appear to know the first thing about building a cabin or growing crops.

The only comment made was by the blacksmith, who remarked the evening after the pair left that they had not been very forthcoming about where they were from, or anything else, for that matter.

Simon and Felicity Ward did not hear of the pair's interest in their valley on their next visit to Bent's Fort. They came once every three months, whether they needed anything or not, principally because Felicity loved to mingle with any women who happened to be there.

On those occasions, Simon would watch over the apple of their eye, their four-and-a-half-year-old son, Peter. The boy was a bubbling fount of childish curiosity who could never sit or stand still for more than a minute. He was always exploring, always venturing places he should not venture, which was why Simon kept a tight rein on him. At Bent's Fort it was safe enough, but elsewhere, even their valley, it was not.

At last count there were eight homesteads along the Front Range and twice that many dotted the nearby prairie. The rest was raw wilderness. Raw, untamed, *savage* wilderness. The land teemed with game, with elk and deer and buffalo and mountain sheep, with squirrel and rabbit and grouse and a variety of waterfowl and fish. And where you found game, you found the meat eaters that preyed on them.

A host of carnivores roamed the mountains and the plains. Huge grizzlies, able to crush a man with a single swipe of a giant paw. Black bears, which generally avoided humans but now and then decided people were as edible as anything else. Mountain lion, wolves, coyotes and foxes—all were plentiful. Wolverines were there, if rare, and most folks were thankful for the rarity. Rattlesnakes were abundant, some as thick as a man's arm, with fearsome fangs that dripped venom.

The beasts were but one peril. Violent men were another. Renegade whites who came to the frontier to evade the law and find new victims. Red men who resented the white influx and counted coup on the invaders.

All perils Simon Ward had to keep in mind.

Thus it was, ten days after he and his loved ones returned to their valley from Bent's Fort, that he stiffened at the drum of hooves in the still of the evening as his family sat at the supper table. He glanced meaningfully at his wife, then dashed to the Hawken rifle he always kept propped near the front door. He took his ammo pouch and powder horn from pegs on the walls and angled them across his chest.

"Douse the lamp," Simon said, moving to the window. It had a glass pane, a luxury Felicity insisted on having but which Simon could have done without. The window was a weak spot. Anyone could break it, and get inside. But he had never refused his wife anything, and when she asked for a real window with real glass instead of a deer hide covering, he had sent all the way to St. Louis for the pane.

Now, careful not to show himself, Simon waited until their cabin was plunged in darkness, then peered out. The sun had set and twilight shrouded the valley.

From the sound, Simon judged that there was one rider. He relaxed a little. A war party would consist of a lot more, and renegade whites tended to travel in packs.

Still, as his mentor and good friend, Nate King, had taught him, it never paid to take anything for granted. Simon placed his thumb on the Hawken's trigger and listened as the rider slowed from a trot to a walk and soon came to a halt right outside.

Both horse and man were big. Uncommonly so. An arm rose in salutation and a deep voice rumbled, "Hello, the cabin! I come in peace!"

Simon hurriedly removed the bar from the door and flung it open. "Nate!" he happily declared as he stepped out into the cool evening air. "This is unexpected. What brings you here?"

The mountain man dismounted. Up close, he was even bigger. He wore buckskins and moccasins, not homespun, like Simon. A walking armory, in addition to a rifle, he was armed with a brace of pistols, a tomahawk, and a bowie knife. His raven hair and beard were neatly trimmed. Piercing green eyes settled on Simon in warm regard, and a grin lit his rugged features. "It is good to see you again, hoss. How is the family?"

"Why don't you come in and see for yourself?" Simon responded, clapping King on the shoulder. "We were just sitting down to eat and would be honored if you would join us."

"Only if you have enough to spare," Nate said. "I won't put that pretty wife of yours to extra bother."

Felicity chose that moment to step to the doorway, young Peter in her arms. "It's no bother to feed you," she said with a smile. She wore a plain dress almost the same color as her sandy hair. "But as it happens, I made plenty. This husband of mine has turned into a bottomless pit. Give him a few years and he'll have a belly."

Nate chuckled and ambled indoors. He had to stoop to clear the lintel. "You know, just because you two are short doesn't mean you should have a doorway fit for midgets."

Simon laughed. He was by no means short. At five feet, ten inches, he was of average height, Felicity a few inches shorter. But Nate was close to seven feet tall, as big a man as Simon ever met. "What about your bay? Can I put it in the corral for you?"

"I won't be staying the night, I am afraid."

Simon hid his disappointment. He and his wife owed their lives to Nate, and Simon regarded him as he would a brother. "We've missed you and your family since you moved. You rode all the way here and can only stay a few minutes?"

"An hour or so," Nate said.

"How is that lovely wife of yours doing?" Felicity asked while lighting the lamp. "And everyone else?"

"Everyone is fine," Nate said. He pulled out a chair and sat. "Winona asked me to relay her regards. Zach and Lou are getting along well." He was referring to his son and daughter-in-law.

"Is Louisa with child yet?" Felicity asked.

"No," Nate answered. "But the way they're making cow eyes at each other, I wouldn't be surprised if it happens any month now."

Simon grinned as he took his usual seat at the

head of the table. "That is young love for you. Our passion rules our heads."

"Is that so?" Felicity asked, blushing.

Nate King folded his big arms over edge of the table. "As for my daughter, Evelyn is being courted."

"No!" Felicity exclaimed in delight. "By whom? Anyone we know?"

"I doubt it," Nate said.

Simon had few dealings with the tribes in the region. Once he had visited Winona King's people, the Shoshones, and been pleasantly delighted by their kindness and courtesy. Each fall a small party of Utes came to his valley for a share of the crops he harvested. It was a special arrangement Nate had worked out. In exchange for part of the farm's bounty, the Utes agreed to let Simon and Felicity live there unmolested.

"Is another marriage in the offing?" Felicity asked,

"Not if Evelyn can help it," Nate said. "She thinks she is too young, and Winona and I agree. She's doing what she can to discourage her suitors, but they are persistent."

"I wish your family had come with you," Felicity said. "I miss them so."

"We've missed you too, but the new valley is beautiful," Nate said. "I've had my fill of cities and towns. Civilization is a cage. Its laws, its rules, pen people in. They have no control. I came to the frontier partly to get away from all that." Nate paused. "But don't get me started or I will go on forever."

"How far is it from here?" Peter asked.

"About a ten-day ride," Nate revealed. "Less if you

push. We wanted to live like we did in the old days, when I first came here. We wanted our privacy back."

"I don't blame you there," Simon commented, which was not entirely true. Unlike Nate, he did not mind people. He had not come West to get away from them. He came for the land, which was there for the taking. He would not mind at all if more homesteaders came. He would not mind if farms sprang up the length and breadth of the land, and if the towns and cities Nate so disliked sprouted along with the crops.

"Nor do I," Felicity said. "It is terrible, the things your family has been through the past couple of years. Those awful men who tried to kill you, and then to have Evelyn kidnapped by that evil Borke woman."

"That wasn't all," Nate said bitterly. "Our old valley had become a stopping point for half the folks heading West, and I was tired of it." He gestured at the window. "It wasn't like here, where you have all the peace and quiet a man could want."

"We're not close to the Oregon Trail, like you were," Simon said. Bent's Fort was only a day and a half ride to the east, but few of the people who stopped there were aware his valley existed.

"You chose well," Nate complimented him. "You are far enough south that the Blackfeet don't bother you, and far enough north that you do not need to worry about the Comanches."

The Blackfeet, as Simon had learned, were the lords of the northern plains. Now and again Blackfoot war parties penetrated into the mountains, into Shoshone and Crow territory, and occasionally, albeit rarely, into the vast domain of the Utes. Their counterparts to the south, the Comanches, were the masters of the southern plains and much of Texas. Other tribes were warlike, and feared, but it was safe to say none were as feared as those two.

Felicity stopped Peter from picking up a knife. "What is this new valley of yours like?"

"It's so remote, no white man has ever set foot in it." Nate said. "Indians shun it because they say it is bad medicine. But you never saw the like! There's more wildlife than you can shake a stick at and plenty of water thanks to a lake fed by a glacier. We will have it all to ourselves, us and the McNairs. It is as close to heaven on earth as this earth ever comes. I love it there."

"We're happy for you," Simon said. But he was not happy for himself and his wife. He was not happy at all. It had been nice having the Kings close. In a crisis, they had always been there to help.

As if Nate King could read Simon's thoughts, he said, "We'll still come on the run if ever you need us. Just because we are a little farther away does not mean we stop being friends."

"That is good to know," Simon said. He did not consider a ten-day ride a "little" farther.

The rest of the meal was devoted to small talk. Afterward, Nate took his leave. He gave Felicity a hug, shook Simon's hand, and climbed on his bay. "Be safe, you two."

His arm around his wife, Simon stood and watched the mountain man vanish into the night. A deep unease gripped him. "I do miss them. We've been very lucky so far."

"We can manage," Felicity said. "We have so far, haven't we?"

"Yes, we have," Simon agreed. He told himself that things would be fine, that he was fretting for no reason.

Not a month later the serpent arrived.

Chapter Two

Felicity Ward was hanging clothes out to dry. It was wash day. She had spent most of the morning at the stream dipping and wringing. She had a large wooden tub but washing the clothes in the stream was easier, and besides, she liked washing outdoors when the weather permitted.

Peter was always with her. He was never out of her sight unless he was with Simon. On this particular morning her husband was off breaking new ground down the valley, backbreaking labor even with the use of a horse-drawn plow.

Felicity was on her knees on a large flat rock, bending to dip one of her bonnets into the cold water, when Peter ran up to her and tugged on her sleeve, squealing in his high-pitched voice, "Men come, Mommy! Men come!"

Instantly, Felicity dropped the bonnet and stood. Strangers were not always friendly, as she and Simon had discovered the hard way. She never went anywhere without her .55-caliber smoothbore pistol, wedged under a belt at her waist, and now she put her hand on it as she turned in the direction her gleeful offspring was pointing.

"Oh, my," Felicity said.

A regular caravan was winding into the east end of their valley, riders and wagons in a long procession that made Felicity think a wagon train had strayed from the Oregon Trail.

Scooping up Peter, Felicity hurried to their cabin. Her rifle was propped within quick reach. Cradling it, she moved over near the chicken coop to better study the newcomers. "Stay behind me," she said to Peter.

"How come?" the boy wanted to know. "Are they bad people?"

Felicity had sat him down one day and did her best to explain to him that the world was filled with basically two kinds of people, the good and the bad. The good were those like the Kings, who never harmed a soul unless they were set upon. The bad were those who hurt out of hate or anger or simply because they liked to inflict pain and suffering, and might want to hurt him. "I don't know yet."

"Father," Peter said.

"He will be all right." Felicity would like to go warn Simon, but she did not dare leave their cabin untended. There was no telling what the strangers might do.

"I see a lady."

So did Felicity, on the seat of the first wagon, her flaxen hair shimmering like straw. That reassured her. Cutthroats seldom traveled with women along. Still, she held her rifle ready to fire it if need be. Not that it would help much if they were up to no good; there were too many. She counted twenty riders, five wagons, and something else.

The something else interested Felicity the most. It was a carriage, a genuine by-God fancy carriage, the likes of which only the rich could afford, pulled by a team of superb white horses. The driver was attired in a red uniform. He wielded a thin whip, cracking it over the heads of the white horses. The whole outfit, riders and wagons, were moving briskly along as if they were in a hurry to get somewhere.

"Pretty horses," Peter said. He was behind her left leg, peering past her dress.

"That they are," Felicity agreed. All the horses were as superb as the whites. She was no judge of horseflesh but she knew enough to recognize superior stock when she saw it.

"What they want?" Peter wondered.

"What *do* they want?" Felicity corrected. "We will find out shortly, I should think."

The caravan was coming toward them. Six of the riders, in pairs, were out in front. Each man was well armed. They wore short-brimmed hats and riding outfits and black boots that came almost to their knees. Lowering her rifle but still with her thumb on the trigger, she took a few steps and smiled in friendly greeting.

One of the lead riders, a square block of a man with muttonchops, returned her smile and waved.

"How do you do?" Felicity called out.

"Never better, thank you, mum," the man answered in a distinct accent she took to be British. "This would be the Ward farm?"

"Yes," Felicity confirmed, still having to holler. "Who might you be?"

The man did not reply. Another did, a tall individual with a severe face and an aloof demeanor, as the party came to a stop. They looked about them with interest. "My name is Severn. This friendly fellow is Mr. Bromley."

"How do you do?" Felicity said.

"A pleasure to make your acquaintance, Mrs. Ward," the cheerful man said.

"We are in the employ of Lord Kilraven," Severn declared, much as someone might say they were in the employ of God Almighty.

"Oh my," Felicity said, and glanced at the carriage with its glittery trappings. "You work for royalty?"

"His lordship is a baron," Severn said. "I oversee a lot of his day-to-day affairs."

"Puff yourself up, why don't you?" Bromley laughed.

Severn's hard face grew harder. "His lordship relies on me to attend to many matters."

"You make a fine spy, I will say that for you," Bromley retorted. "Why did you ask this lady if this was the Ward farm when you bloody well know it is?"

"Watch your tongue," Severn said harshly.

A man behind them coughed. He had drooping jowls that lent him a perpetually sad expression. "Both of you had better watch them or his lordship will hear about your little spat."

Severn seemed disposed to argue, but a yell from the flaxen-haired woman on the first wagon threw a bucket of water on his fiery temper.

"What is this, then? Are you going to sit there talking all day when Lord Kilraven has made it clear he wants to pitch camp by four o'clock?"

"We better push on," Severn said.

Bromley touched his hat brim to Felicity and smiled. "Our apologies, mum. We do not mean to be unsociable, but we must press on or there will be the very devil to pay."

"I hope my husband and I will get to see all of you again," Felicity said in earnest. She did not like the cold look Severn shot her or understand its significance.

"There is no doubt of that, Mrs. Ward," Bromley said. "There is no doubt of that at all."

One by one the wagons and the carriage rattled and creaked past. Felicity hoped for a glimpse of his lordship, but the curtains were drawn against the heat and the dust. She had to settle for a nod from the driver in red.

"Are they good people, Mother?" Peter asked as the riders who brought up the rear went by. The last man held the lead rope to a long string of pack animals.

"I am sure they are," Felicity said.

Simon Ward had been toiling for hours now. Stripped to the waist, his rifle and pistols on a stump bordering the field, he bent to the plow and shouted at his plow horse, "On, Dancer, on!" Simon had named him Dancer because of the way he pranced when he was excited, as when Simon treated him to a carrot or sugar. Dancer was a Belgian draft horse, a breed noted for their huge muscles and prodigious strength. A giant, Dancer measured sixty-five inches at the shoulders and weighed in excess of seventeen hundred pounds. And he was worth every ounce in the amount of work he did without tiring.

It was pushing two in the afternoon, judging by the position of the sun, when Simon happened to glance in the direction of his cabin and barn. He was thinking of Felicity and their son, of how much he loved them, of how in all the world, they meant the most to him. He could not see the buildings; they were too far off. But he did behold a sight that nearly startled the wits out of him.

"What in the world?" he blurted.

Simon stared in amazement as a wagon train came winding up his valley. So many people. So many wagons, and even a carriage that reminded him of some he had seen in Boston, where he was born and raised. He was so amazed that he almost forgot about his rifle and pistols. Almost. The lead riders were two hundred yards away when Simon went to the stump, donned the shirt Felicity had crafted for him with her own hands, and armed himself with his rifle and pistols. Then he stood by Dancer and the plow, and waited.

Of the four lead riders, only one seemed hostile and did not smile when a man named Bromley introduced them.

"You are English, unless I miss my guess," Simon said.

"We are Brits," the hostile one, Severn, said. "Any twit could tell that."

Bromley shifted in his English-style saddle. "Enough, if you please. His lordship has not given permission for you to vent your spleen quite yet." He smiled down at Simon. "I am sorry. He tends to speak his mind without thinking."

"Bloody hell," Severn said.

"Where are you bound, if you do not mind my asking?" Simon was curious to learn. "West of here is nothing but wilderness and more wilderness."

Bromley pointed at a large flat-topped hill at the west end of the valley. "We reckon to camp there for the night."

"And tomorrow?" Simon asked.

"Each day takes care of itself, eh?" Bromley said enigmatically. "I am sorry, but we really must be going. We have tents to pitch and fires to make."

"Nice meeting you," Simon said.

Severn laughed.

They rode on, and after them lumbered the wagons. A woman with yellow hair gave Simon a polite nod. Few of the men so much as glanced at him. Then came the expensive carriage. It was abreast of him when, on an impulse, Simon yelled, "Lord Kilraven! Do you have a moment?"

Apparently he did not because the carriage went on by. The driver in red glanced at Simon and then at the side of the carriage as if awaiting a command, and when none came, he shrugged and flicked his long whip at the team of white horses.

Simon was disappointed. He would have liked to meet a British lord. In Boston the British Parliament and royalty were often mentioned in the newspaper. He had been taught a little about the British system of government in school, but he would be hanged if he could remember much of it.

The last of the riders faded into the dust. Simon took off his shirt and placed his weapons on the stump and went back to work. There was plenty of daylight left and he had a lot more ground to till.

As he worked, Simon wondered about the gentleman in the carriage. He supposed the lord was doing what many of the rich and powerful were doing those days, and had ventured West for a few weeks of adventure and thrills. Nate King had mentioned a senator who showed up at Bent's Fort on a buffalo hunt, and there had been a wealthy plantation owner from North or South Carolina who came to the Rockies to hunt mountain sheep, of all things.

To have more money than Midas, that was the life, Simon reflected. He'd never had much money, himself. His job as a clerk at a mercantile had barely paid enough for the necessities, let alone luxuries. But he had scrimped and saved, and combined with the bit of money Felicity had socked away, they had sufficient funds to buy a wagon and come to the frontier. He could never thank her enough for that. Without her, his dream would still be just that.

His family had been against the idea. Felicity's, too, at first. They would be killed, everyone warned. Hostiles were everywhere, and the land was overrun with wild beasts. But as in most things in life, people exaggerated. Yes, there were hostile tribes, but there were a lot of friendly tribes, too, and so long as a man knew who was who and shied away from territory roamed by the hostile variety, he did not need to worry much about losing his hair. And yes, the wilds teemed with beasts of all kinds, but the predators mostly did their hunting at night. Mountain lions and wolves tended to leave people alone, and black bears almost always ran at the sight of a human being. That left grizzlies, the lords of the mountains and plains. Simon had been fortunate in that he had encountered only a few, and those few had no interest in devouring him.

He was fortunate in another regard, as well. Nate told him once that back in the early days grizzlies were everywhere. A man could not turn around without bumping into one. The trappers who followed the waterways deep into the mountains after beaver plews were frequently attacked, and paid for their temerity in invading the grizzly's domain with maimed bodies and crippled limbs. A lot of those grizzlies had been killed off.

Dancer's lengthening shadow brought Simon out of his reverie. The sun was dipping toward the western horizon. Shielding his eyes with a hand, he saw that the wagons had reached the flat-topped hill. Antlike figures were scurrying about, setting up camp.

Only then did it occur to Simon that Lord Kilraven had not asked his permission to cross his valley. Unless, Simon reflected, Kilraven had asked it of Felicity.

Felicity. Simon gazed to the east. Suddenly he wanted to be home, to see her and hold her, and be with Peter. He unhooked the plow and left it there. No one would bother it. Indians had no use for plows, and the only white men within miles were the lord's party. They hardly had use for it, either.

Leading Dancer, Simon started back. "You did

good today, my wonderful Samson," he said. "You are the best investment I ever made." He meant it. Without Dancer's tireless efforts, the farm would not be half as big as it was. A lesser plow horse could not have done nearly as much.

Now, gazing out across acre after acre of tilled soil, the crops growing green in the rosy glow of the setting sun, Simon swelled with pride. Long, hard hours had gone into wresting a living from the un-yielding earth. He had known from the outset how hard it would be, far harder than making his living as a clerk. But anything worthwhile, as his mother liked to say, was worth extra effort.

Simon glanced over his shoulder and frowned. He did not have it easy, like that lord. He would never have it easy. But he would not trade his life for all the finery in Merry Old England.

Simon was happy. He was content. All was well with his world, and he prayed it would stay that way.

Chapter Three

Felicity was chopping green beans and dropping them in a pot she had set on the stove to boil. Simon was in a chair at the table, bouncing a giggling Peter on his knees. Hoofbeats caused both of them to stop and perk their ears.

"We have a visitor," Felicity stated the obvious.

"Only one rider," Simon said. He held Peter out and she quickly came and took him, freeing Simon to arm himself with his rifle and open the door a few inches. He was careful not to show himself.

"Hallo, the cabin! I come in peace."

Simon opened the door wider. In the gathering twilight he recognized Bromley, the friendly one. "What can we do for you?"

"On behalf of Lord Kilraven, I am to invite you to supper at our encampment," Bromley requested. "He apologizes for the lateness of the hour and the tardy invitation, but it took longer than we anticipated to set things in order."

"It is late," Simon said, and glanced at Felicity. They rarely went abroad after dark. "What do you say, dearest?"

Felicity had already taken the pot off the stove. "Need you ask? Pass up a chance to meet a real lord?"

Bromley laughed. "His lordship is looking forward to having words with you two, as well."

Simon hitched up the buckboard. He had bought it the year before, and relied on it almost as much as he did Dancer. It was ideal for hauling everything from the rocks and boulders he dug out of the ground, to harvested crops. He folded a blanket and placed it on the seat for Felicity's benefit, then brought the buckboard from the barn to the cabin.

Felicity was ready to go. She had on her best dress and her best bonnet, and was holding Peter. "Mr. Bromley was just telling me about their voyage to America, and how they spent the better part of the last two months in St. Louis."

"Why there?" Simon asked the Brit.

"We were awaiting word in regards to a certain enterprise his lordship has in mind," Bromley said. He glanced toward the lights atop the distant hill. "I don't mean to hurry you, but Lord Kilraven will be waiting."

Simon held Peter while Felicity climbed up; then he handed Peter to her and swung onto the seat. Out of habit they had brought brought their rifles. He leaned his against his leg and worked the reins. "Get along there!"

Bromley brought his horse alongside. "Do you like it out here, Mr. Ward?" he asked.

"I would not live anywhere else," Simon answered.

"Living all alone as you do?" Bromley said. He idly tugged at a muttonchop. "I don't know as I would. Not with a family. There is a lot of danger, is there not? We have heard a lot of stories about the savages and the vicious beasts."

"Anywhere you live has its dangers," Simon countered. "You can be run over by a wagon in the heart of any city. Or be knifed or shot."

"True," the Brit conceded. "But the odds of that are small. Out here, painted devils are common, I hear, and animals are everywhere."

"We have lived here six years now and are still alive."

"That long? I did not realize." Bromley was quiet a bit, then, "Still, it would be better for your family, I should think, if you were back in civilization."

Felicity cleared her throat. "Speaking on my own behalf, I am perfectly content to live out the rest of my life right where we are. I could not imagine a more glorious life."

Bromley looked at her. "Glorious? Isn't that an exaggeration?"

"Not at all," Felicity said. "Oh, the work is hard. I don't deny that. But by glorious I mean having the freedom to live as we please, with no one telling us what to do."

"You sound like Nate King," Simon teased.

"What about the culture civilization has to offer?" Bromley pressed them. "The theater. Places to dine. Being able to buy whatever you need at the market. Don't you miss any of that?"

"Not at all," Felicity assured him.

Bromley sighed. "I am sorry to hear that. I truly am."

"Why should you be sorry?" Simon wondered.

"Oh, no reason. Except that it has to be rough on your wife and the lad, no matter what she says."

"I do not make a habit of lying," Felicity told him.

"I am sure you do not. No insult intended, Mrs. Ward," Bromley said. He clucked to his horse and rode on ahead, following the rutted tracks left by the wagons, which were plainly visible in the light of the full moon.

"A gorgeous night," Felicity said, admiring the celestial spectacle.

"Yes, it is," Simon agreed. But he was not looking at the stars. He was thinking of what their escort had said.

Campfires blazed atop the hill. The kind of campfires Nate King would call a white man's fire. "You can usually tell who has made a fire by how big or small it is," he imparted to Simon years ago. "Indians make their fire small so it will not be spotted by their enemies. White men make a big fire because they are scared of the dark."

Simon had chuckled and said, "Be serious. Men our age do not live in fear of hobgoblins. We build big fires because we like to see what we are doing, and for the heat they give off."

"Tell that to the Blackfoot who lifts your scalp."

The climb up the hill took a while. The slope was steep until near the top, where a fluke of geology had resulted in a flat crown some four acres in extent. The wagons were parked in a semicircle, a barrier, such as it was, between the lord's party and whatever lurked in the inky wilds beyond. The carriage was next to a large tent. Other tents had been erected a stone's throw away.

Simon was impressed to see that sentries had been posted. One came out of the dark and watched the buckboard go by.

"You are very well organized," Simon said to Bromley.

"His lordship would not have it any other way."

A long table had been placed near the fire closest to Lord Kilraven's tent. Chairs had been set out, and silverware and glasses arranged.

"My goodness!" Felicity marveled as Simon brought the buckboard to a halt. "You had all that in your wagons?"

"And a lot more," Bromley replied.

A man in an apron was busy cooking. A pert brunette in what could only be a maid's uniform was carrying a pitcher of water to the table.

"He even brought his servants?" Simon said as he helped his wife down.

"His lordship would not think of going anywhere without his personal staff," Bromley revealed. "The same with her ladyship."

"Lord Kilraven brought his wife?" Simon was mildly taken aback. After all of Bromley's talk about the dangers of the frontier, it surprised him that the lord had brought his lady.

"His lordship never goes anywhere without her. They are inseparable," Bromley informed them. "She has been with him to India and Africa, and to the islands of the Caribbean."

"I envy her," Felicity said. "I have always yearned to see more of the world."

"Perhaps you will have that chance."

"I doubt it," Felicity said. "I cannot afford to be away from home for more than a week or two at a time. The work would pile up to where I would be swamped when I got back."

"You never know," Bromley said cryptically.

At that juncture Severn appeared. "About time," he griped. "His lordship is growing impatient."

"We came straight away," Bromley said.

"By way of Canada, no doubt. His lordship said he will talk with you later." Severn beckoned to the Wards. "This way, if you please. As soon as you are seated, Lord Kilraven will join you."

Simon felt he should say something in Bromley's defense. "We came as fast as the buckboard permitted." Without goading the team into a gallop, which he was not about to do with his wife and son along.

"I am sure, sir," Severn said, with a tone and an air that indicated he did not really care.

Simon would not let it rest. "Tell me," he said, looping an arm around Felicity's waist. "Do you dislike all Americans or just us?"

Severn looked back at them, his countenance sculpted from ice. "I have nothing against any of you provincials, sir, other than you *are* provincials."

"Provincials?" Felicity said.

When Severn did not respond, Bromley said, "It is a term some of us apply to anyone from the colonies. It suggests they lack a certain refinement or polish."

"I implied no such thing," Severn quickly said. "I would never presume to insult his lordship's guests."

"You better not," Simon said. He had decided he disliked the man, intensely. "Or we will take our leave and you can tell Lord Kilraven we left because of your bad manners."

Severn colored from collar to hair line. "I am sorry if you took offense, sir. Again, no slur was intended."

"We will overlook it, this time," Felicity intervened. She was worried her husband would become mad and want to leave, depriving her of the one and only chance in her lifetime to rub elbows with English aristocracy. "But I am puzzled. Why does he call us the colonies? The United States broke away from Britain seventy-five years ago."

"Some of us still regard your country as the colonies, Mrs. Ward," Severn said with studied politeness. "We have always thought your revolution was misguided."

"My grandfather fought in that revolution," Simon brought up. "He always told me it had to be done, that King George overstepped himself. I would not call opposing tyranny misguided."

Severn made as if to reply, but Bromley hastily said, "I doubt his lordship would be pleased by this discussion. Save the politics for another time."

"Very well," Severn said. "His lordship's interests always come before our own."

Simon wondered what the man meant by that. He was not given much chance to ponder, as a second later the flap to the large tent parted and out emerged a lovely young woman who had to be all of sixteen years old. Her luxurious black hair was done in lustrous curls, and she wore an exquisite dress that flared wide from her slender waist down. It swished as she walked. "Did I hear someone mention politics? I hope not, because I would be hard pressed to think of anything that bores me more."

Bromley dipped in a slight bow, saying, "Mr. and Mrs. Ward, permit me to introduce Lord Kilraven's niece, Cadena Taylor. Her father is Lady Saxona's brother."

"Lady Saxona is Lord Kilraven's wife?" Felicity asked.

Cadena put her hands on her hips. "Haven't you told them *anything*?" she demanded of Bromley and Severn.

"Only what we were told to say," Severn replied. "No more."

Scowling, Cadena came over to the Wards. "Please forgive their lack of courtesy. Menials can be that way, you know." She smiled at Felicity. "Yes, Saxona is Lord Kilraven's wife, and my aunt. She was gracious enough to permit me to come along."

"Have you enjoyed your time in our country?" Felicity asked. She could not get over how magnificent the girl's dress was, and how beautifully her hair had been done. Suddenly Felicity was acutely conscious of her drab homespun, and how her hair must look in comparison.

"Oh, yes, it has been quite marvelous," Cadena said. "The way Americans dress, the way they talk, you are all so natural and uninhibited."

"More of that provincialism," Simon remarked.

"Excuse me?"

"Mr. Severn mentioned that many of your countrymen regard us as provincials," Simon elaborated.

"Mr. Severn should be whipped," Cadena said. "I prefer to think of your country as possessing a certain charm and vitality."

From the front of the big tent came an imperious, "Is that so, my dear?". The voice brought to Simon's mind the image of fingernails on a chalkboard. He turned, along with the rest.

Her posture and bearing positively regal, a wisp of a woman with an extremely pale complexion flowed toward them. Her stick frame was arrayed in the finest dress money could obtain, her gray-brown hair was the height of European coiffure, her shoes gleamed with polish. She held her right hand limply in front of her, as if groping for invisible support.

"Lady Saxona!" Severn blurted.

"You were expecting the queen, perhaps?" Saxona bitingly retorted, and wriggled her limp fingers. "Off you go. You, too, Mr. Bromley. Cadena and I will attend to our visitors."

"As you wish, my lady," Severn said, bowing.

Saxona waited until the two men were out of earshot, then remarked, "I do so loathe the servile slug, but what is a person to do? The quality of help these days leaves a lot to be desired."

"I have never had that problem," Felicity joked, and when the other woman looked at her in apparent confusion, she said, "I could never afford a maid, let alone manservants."

"Ah," Saxona said. "I have only two maids with me, and they are nowhere near enough." She indicated the flaxen-haired woman in uniform at the table. "That is Fayre. She has been with me the longest, and is quite good at anticipating my needs. But the other one, Wenda—" She stopped and shook her head.

"Now, now, auntie," Cadena said. "Please don't start in on the hired help. Our guests will think us perfect bores."

"We would not want that, would we?" Saxona asked, and laughed merrily, much more merrily than the comment warranted. "Now suppose we take our seats? My husband will join us directly."

Simon held out a chair for Felicity and she sat, Peter in her arms. He dropped into the one next to hers. "Is Lord Kilraven here to hunt game?" he inquired of Saxona as she claimed the seat at the end of the table to his left.

"Oh, no, Mr. Ward. My husband has much loftier ambitions. He is here to find land. A great lot of land."

Chapter Four

As they made more small talk, a distinct uneasiness gripped Simon Ward and would not relent. He could not say why.

Then the tent flap parted and out came their host.

Lord Kilraven was a striking individual. Exceedingly tall, he very nearly rivaled Nate King in height. But where the mountain man was a living wall of muscle, Lord Kilraven was a walking cadaver. Hideously thin, to the point where he appeared to literally be skin and bones, his lordship was further distinguished by a mane of snow white hair. He was not fussy about brushing or combing it, and tufts stuck out here and there, lending him an unkempt aspect that belied his cultured status. His clothes, as with those of his wife and niece, were the absolute best of the current vogue in fashion. Where on other men his clothes would add to their appeal, on Lord Kilraven the fine knee-length coat and white shirt and striped pants seemed oddly out of place, as if a walking corpse had been decked out for burial.

Kilraven's face did not help matters. His lordship had a high forehead, bushy white eyebrows that were perpetually arched, high cheekbones, a thin slit of a mouth, and, most prominent of all, a hooked nose that reminded one of the beak of a bird of prey. His eyes were a piercing gray.

A tight smile lifting the corners of his lips, the British peer advanced with a bony hand out-stretched. "Mr. and Mrs. Ward. It is a pleasure to meet you at last. I have heard a great deal about you and your valley."

"You have?" Simon responded. The strength in the man's grip surprised him.

Felicity was amused when Kilraven delicately clasped her fingers, bowed, and pressed them to his lips. Their touch was fleeing, and so cold the sensation sent a tiny shiver down her spine. "You are the first royalty I have ever met."

Lord Kilraven assumed the seat at the other end of the table, a chair, Simon noted, with the highest back and the widest seat, and an engraved crest. It made Simon think of a throne.

"Do not make overmuch of my status, my good lady. I am a baron, true, but there are big barons and there are little barons, and I am very much of the tri-fling variety."

"Such modesty," Felicity said by way of praise.

"Not really," Lord Kilraven said. "I am practical by nature, and practicality demands the truth. But enough of me. The hour is late and you must be fam-ished. I propose we eat, then discuss the purpose for my visit to your country, which you will very much want to hear." He clapped his hands, and the maids and other servants materialized and began bringing silver trays heaped high with food, and china bowls filled with simmering soups and broths.

It was spectacular, the lengths they had gone to. There was venison, buffalo and elk and grouse, so much they could never eat it all, along with potatoes and vegetables and British dishes they sampled for the novelty, including a pie with meat in it and pudding mixed with bread.

While they ate, the lord talked about life in England, and the voyage to America. He did not eat a lot, himself, which accounted for his cadaverous appearance.

"I am grateful you accepted my invitation. Please do not be offended, but I have found manners singularly lacking among your countrymen. Proper behavior seems to have fallen by the wayside when America cast off British rule."

"We are not sticklers over how to do things," Felicity said while eating with Peter perched in her lap. "We do them as we please."

"So I have noticed, my good woman," Lord Kilraven said. "As countries go, you are new and unlettered, and that accounts for part of it. But please do not get the impression I dislike America. Far from it. I see it as a land of marvelous opportunity, especially in the making of that which your countrymen esteem above all else."

"Money?" Simon guessed.

Lord Kilrane nodded. "I have never been anywhere where money is so coveted. Oh, riches are sought by everyone with common sense, but in America becoming rich seems to be the ambition of every man I meet."

"Men long for what they don't have," Simon remarked offhandedly.

"That they do," Lord Kilraven concurred. "I can apply that to myself, for I constantly long to better my station financially. You might deem that simple greed, but if I increase my wealth, I can go from being a little baron to a big baron, to being a man of power and influence. That, to me, is the heady wine that makes existence worthwhile."

"Power?" Felicity said.

"Yes, my dear. You have men of power in this country, do you not? Your president and your senators and what have you. Men who dictate how those under them should live."

Simon lowered his fork. "It doesn't quite work that way over here, your lordship. They are accountable to the people. We vote them into office and we can just as easily vote them out again."

"A quibble, my good sir," Kilraven said. "For once in office, they can do as they please. And once there, so long as they grease the wheel back home, as a congressman explained it to me, they stay in office for as long as they desire." He snapped his fingers and a servant appeared and filled his crystal glass with wine. Raising the glass to his nose, he sniffed, then took a sip. "Power is very much its own reward."

Simon was gazing about the encampment. Most of the men bristled with weapons. Kilraven had brought a small army, enough to discourage most hostiles from attacking. The majority of those not on sentry duty were seated around the campfires, eating and conversing in low tones.

"There are various ways of acquiring power," Lord Kilraven was saying. "Power can be inherited, as is the case with many of my countrymen. Or power can be acquired through diligent effort. Or a combination of both."

"You seem to be quite fascinated by it," Felicity commented, more to hold up their end of the conversation than out of any genuine interest. She had the impression Kilraven was talking down to them, treating them as the provincials Severn had mentioned, and she resented it. She told herself it must be her imagination, that Kilraven was acting as he would with anyone, but his next comment proved her intuition right.

"I am indeed. I would be remiss were I not," Kilraven said. "Another reason those in power here find it easy to keep that power, I would imagine, is that those they have power over are ignorant of its subtleties. They can be handled much as a sheepherder handles his sheep."

"People aren't sheep," Simon said flatly. "If you think they are, then you know nothing about America or Americans."

Both Saxona and Cadena stirred in their chairs and cast glances at Kilraven but he merely smiled his thin smile.

"A matter of opinion, I daresay. In any event, the important thing is that power must be wielded with an iron fist or there is no use having it."

"King George tried the iron fist on us and look where it got him," Simon observed.

Lord Kilraven frowned. "He was a fool for letting the colonies slip from his grasp. Had I been in his position, I would have brought the full might of the British empire to bear to crush the revolution, and I would have sentenced all those involved to the gallows."

"You would have tried," Simon said.

Lord Kilraven sat back and draped his spindly arms over the arms of his thronelike chair. "I do so hope you are not one of those who fancies he can resist the inevitable."

"I am a simple man, with simple means, making a living the best I know how."

Saxona Kilraven broke her long silence with, "Your family means a great deal to you, does it not?"

"My family is everything to me," Simon admitted. "I love my wife and my son more than anything."

"I am happy for you, sir," Lord Kilraven said. "Although I must confess I find love overrated."

Felicity was appalled. To her there was no greater emotion. Her love for her husband and her son was the sum and substance of her existence. "In what way overrated?"

"Several ways," his lordship answered. "For one, it is never as grand nor as glorious as the poets would have us believe. We fall in love, but what is love, really, other than the brief stirring of passion?"

"There is more to love than that," Felicity responded. "I love Simon for the man he is inside."

Simon smiled at her.

"Oh, granted, that is an element," Lord Kilraven conceded. "But after a while it tends to wane. Familiarity breeds, if not contempt, then the realization that the one we adore is not nearly as adorable as we first imagined them to be."

Amazed that Kilraven would utter a comment like that with his wife sitting right there, Felicity said, "My husband is every bit as adorable today as he was the day we were wed."

"Give yourself a few more years, my dear," Lord Kilraven said. "But the point I was trying to make is that in the scheme of things, love should not be first and foremost. Love is fragile. Love is uncertain. Only power endures."

Felicity shifted toward their hostess. "And you, Lady Kilraven? Do you share your husband's outlook?"

Saxona glanced at Kilraven, who nodded. "To a degree," she said guardedly. "Our marriage was what you Americans might call a marriage of convenience. His family and mine can trace their bloodlines back many generations. It was unthinkable to marry someone below our mutual stations."

"Are you saying that you married him because of what he is rather than the person he is?"

"That is exactly what I am saying, yes," Saxona confirmed. "I would never stoop to wedding, say, a simple stone mason, or a clerk."

"I was a clerk once," Simon said.

"A worthwhile profession, don't get me wrong. But it can hardly compare to the social status of a peer of the realm. Had Laurence not been a baron, I would not have given him the time of day." Saxona put a hand to her lips. "Oh. I am sorry, husband. I know you do not like having your first name used."

"That is all right," Lord Kilraven said, his tone

suggesting it was anything but. "But all this talk of love is straying us off the mark. I would rather discuss why we are here."

"Please do, then," Saxona said.

Clearing his throat, Kilraven gazed down the benighted valley. "As I mentioned a while ago, America is a boundless land of opportunity. There are fortunes to be made here, many and diverse, and I would very much like to make my own."

"But you are a lord," Felicity said.

"Implying I should have more money than I could possibly need?" Kilraven rather sadly shook his head. "That is not how it works. Just as there are little barons and big barons, there are rich ones and poor ones. I am, much to my shame, more poor than rich. Oh, I have a large estate, and the trappings that go with my title. But I can barely afford them."

"I had no idea," Simon said. The fine clothes, the crystal and china, the carriage, had all given the impression the Kilravens were fabulously wealthy.

"Oh, yes," Lord Kilraven said. "To give you some idea, at my estate I have eleven servants. Lord Cushing has twenty-seven. Lord Thackery has thirty-nine. Granted, their estates are larger, but you see my point."

"You hope to have more."

"With money I can. With enough money I can do anything," Kilraven declared. "Which is why I have been casting about for some time, seeking the ideal means to amass the wealth that is my due. The opportunities over here were brought to my attention by friends and associates who have invested in American enterprises and reaped huge rewards."

"Your wife mentioned that you hope to acquire a lot of land," Felicity commented.

"Did she indeed?"

"I meant no harm," Saxona quickly said.

"Be that as it may, you really must learn when to speak and when not to." Kilraven drummed his fingers on the table, then shrugged. "Oh, well. Yes, Mrs. Ward, land is important to my plans. But only to the extent that from the land shall come the spoils."

"How is that again?"

Kilraven made a teepee of his slender fingers. "What do my countrymen and yours have in common? Don't answer. I will tell you. They are sportsmen. They love to hunt. We have fox hunts and stag hunts. You have every type of game animal conceivable. Fowl for the bird hunter, deer and bison and antelope for those who like bigger game, and for those who savor the spice of danger, wolves and panthers and bears. Something for everyone."

"I would avoid the bears were I you," Simon advised.

Kilraven did not seem to hear him. "Most of the hunting in my country is done on hunting preserves, and because the preserves are stocked with game, the success rate is quite high. Here, a man can hunt just about anywhere, but it is a hit-or-miss affair. Some days a hunter is lucky, other days he is not."

"True," Simon said. "I can't tell you how many times I have come home empty-handed."

"I propose to remedy that. I intend to establish and operate a hunting preserve here in America. The largest preserve in the world. Game will be

herded or driven or caught and brought to the preserve by my attendants, so that everyone who hunts
will be assured of success. For that privilege, and
the privilege of staying at the hunting lodge I plan
to build, they will pay, and pay handsomely."

"That is a brilliant idea," Felicity said.

"I thought so, too," Kilraven said. "My first step,
then, is to acquire the land for the preserve. Where
better than on the frontier, where game animals are
so abundant? I calculate that a hundred of your
square miles should be sufficient."

Simon whistled.

"That is a considerable amount of land," Felicity
observed. "Do you have an area picked out?"

"As a matter of fact, I do." Lord Kilraven smiled.
"You are sitting in the center of it."

"Pardon?"

"Your valley, Mrs. Ward. I hereby claim it for my
own."

Chapter Five

Felicity Ward had never heard anything so preposterous in her life. "But we live here. This valley is ours. We would never give it up."

"Your wishes are irrelevant," Lord Kilraven said. "I have made up my mind. I will, of course, reimburse you for the money you have invested in your homestead. A fair price, at my discretion."

Felicity looked at Saxona and Cadena, neither of whom would meet her gaze. "You knew about this?"

"My husband does not keep secrets from me," Lady Kilraven said.

"And you?" Felicity said to his niece.

"I am sorry. There is nothing I can do. I am underage, and at any rate, his lordship does as he sees fit." Cadena squirmed in her seat. "Now that I have met you, I find I like you. I would talk him out of it if I could, but I can't, so why bother?"

Lord Kilraven was staring fixedly at Simon. "You

have been strangely silent during this exchange, Mr. Ward. Have you no sentiment to express?"

Simon had been silent, all right, because he was boiling with anger. That his earlier unease had been justified and was not a paranoid phantom of his mind was no consolation. "There are a few things I would like to know before I give you my reply."

"Certainly," Lord Kilraven said.

"Why *our* valley? The Rockies run from Canada to Mexico. There are as many valleys as stars in the sky. Why pick *ours*, damn you?"

Kilraven leaned his elbows on the table. "Now, now. Let's not have any of that, shall we? We can keep a civil tongue, if nothing else." He sniffed. "As for the why of it, your valley offers advantages I can not ignore. Your stream flows all year long, I understand, unlike a lot of streams in this region which dry up during the summer. Water is crucial. My hunting lodge will be the largest of its kind. Its staff and the people who come to hunt will need a continual supply."

"There is a river fifty miles to the north. It has all the water you could need."

"But for most of its length it passes through a narrow channel," Lord Kilraven said. "And the hunting there is poor, I am told. No, I considered it, but it will not do."

"What other advantages does our valley offer?" Simon asked. He had a fair idea but he wanted to hear it from Kilraven.

"Second after the water is its proximity to Bent's Fort, the only trading post in a thousand miles. I require a relay point for the items I will send for, and a source of provisions. Bent's Fort serves both needs adequately."

"Anything else?"

"The Indians here are not as inimical to whites as elsewhere. To the north are the Blackfeet. They come down this way but only occasionally. To the northeast are the Sioux, who seldom come this far. The nearby Utes are not always friendly, but neither are they openly hostile unless provoked." His lordship smiled. "You see, I have done my homework, as they say."

"Is that all?" Simon coldly asked.

Kilraven thought a moment. "One last factor is worthy of mention, and in one respect it is the most essential." He nodded toward the towering peaks to the west. "These mountains teem with game. Countless deer and hundreds of elk are within a few days ride. To say nothing of the mountain buffalo and mountain sheep I hear inhabit the forests and the rocky heights, respectively. Then there are the grouse and quail. On a lake to the northwest ducks and geese abound. Enough game for hundreds of hunts, and at the prices I will charge, enough for me to reap a fortune."

Simon became aware he was still holding his spoon. He set it down next to his plate and lowered his hand under the table to a pistol. "Surely you can't think I will let you take the valley away from us?"

"You are one man. I have many and can send for many more. I don't see how you can possibly stop me."

Felicity had listened to enough. "We settled here

first," she angrily declared. "You can't just waltz in and take it."

"My dear women, that is exactly what I *can* do," Lord Kilraven responded. "You forget. You have no bona fide legal claim. Oh, you settled here, but you have never filed on the land. You have never registered it in your name."

"But we can't!" Felicity exclaimed in rising horror as the full significance hit her.

Kilraven smirked at the irony. "No, you cannot. Simply because you are so far removed from civilization, there is no government. No towns. No cities. No counties, I believe you call them. No local, state, or federal authorities. No oversight. No legal guarantees. You are entirely on your own. The valley is yours only so long as you can hold on to it."

Felicity did not know what to think. It was all so sudden. "This can't be happening," she said, more to herself than anyone else.

Simon wanted to take her in his arms and assure her everything would be all right, but he had never lied to her and would not start now. "I will fight you, Lord Kilraven. I will resist you any way I can."

His lordship drained his glass of wine and slowly set it down. "I had hoped you would be more receptive. But if I were in your shoes, I would probably feel the same way. I regret the steps I must now take but you leave me with no choice." He gestured imperiously. "Mr. Severn, if you please."

Something hard touched the nape of Simon's neck. Instinctively, he started to unlimber his pistol but froze when he heard the rasp of a gun hammer being pulled back.

"I wouldn't, Yank, were I you," the man called Severn warned. "One twitch of my finger and this rifle is liable to go off. You wouldn't want the misses and your brat to see your head blown off, would you?"

"Disarm him," Lord Kilraven commanded.

Bromley and two others appeared on each side of Simon's chair. The former stood scowling while the other two separated Simon from his weapons, even his knife, and stepped back.

"Disarm the woman, too."

Felicity was nearly beside herself. She wanted to resist, but what could she do with her child in her lap? She sat still as they relieved her of her means of defending herself. "What now?" she bitterly asked. "Will you have us murdered?"

"Nothing so extreme, I assure you," Kilraven said smugly. "I will give you three days to pack whatever personal effects you care to take. Four days from now, at eight in the morning, some of my men will be at your cabin to escort you to Bent's Fort. From there you are on your own."

"I will tell everyone what you have done to us," Simon vowed. "There will be hell to pay."

"From whom? The Bent brothers? St. Vrain? They are businessmen. They care about their trading post, nothing else."

"If you make me leave, I will come back," Simon said. "I will find a way to stop you."

"Spare me your braggadocio," Kilraven said. "Accept the inevitable and get on with your life."

"Like hell," Simon indulged in a rare curse. "I have years of labor and sweat invested in our homestead. I will not let you or anyone else steal it out from under us."

"I offered to compensate you," Kilraven said. "Name your price, and so long as it is fair, it is yours."

"You are a dead man," Simon Ward said.

Fear welled in Felicity. It occurred to her that if her husband made Kilraven mad, it could get ugly, and he was hopelessly outnumbered. "Simon," she said tentatively. "Maybe we should just do as he wants for now."

Heedless of the men who hemmed him, Simon rose, leaned on the table, and glared at Laurence Kilraven. "Do what you will, but I will resist you with my dying breath."

"Be reasonable," Saxona Kilraven interjected.

"*Reasonable?*" Simon exploded, and pounded the table with his fist. "You come in here, you threaten to throw us out of our home and seize our land, and you want me to be *reasonable*? Are you insane?"

Lord Kilraven let out a long, loud sigh. "I had hoped you would be sensible about this. After all, is it really that terrible an inconvenience? You can take the money I give you and start over. It is not as if I am casting you out penniless."

"You *are* insane," Simon said.

"No, I am a man accustomed to getting what he wants, and unfortunately for you, I want this valley." Lord Kilraven rose. "I can see that further discussion is pointless. You are burning with wrath and not thinking properly. Tomorrow, if you have a clearer head, we can talk again."

"I will feel the same tomorrow as I do right now," Simon snapped.

"That is a pity. It has been my experience that business arrangements are best conducted when cool heads prevail."

"Is that what this is to you? You trample people under your heel and call it business?"

"Call it whatever you like," Lord Kilraven said. "Just so you realize that resisting is futile. My men will have you under constant watch from this moment on. Try anything, anything at all, and it will be to your great regret."

Felicity was fighting back tears. "And here I looked forward to meeting you! A baron, no less! A real, honest-to-God lord! I imagined you as noble, as a living example of all that is good and decent, but you are a common thief who just happens to have a title."

"Enough." Kilraven wheeled and waved a hand. "Mr. Severn, you know what to do. Take Bromley and four or five others, and leave someone to keep watch near their cabin."

"As you will, sir."

Kilraven paused at the large tent, the flap partway open, and glanced over his shoulder. "We can do this easy or we can do this hard, Mr. and Mrs. Ward. We can do it with no suffering on your part, or with a lot of suffering on your part. The choice is yours. Choose wisely."

Simon was not a violent man. He rarely became mad, truly mad, and could count on one hand and have fingers to spare the number of times he had yearned to hurt someone. But he keenly yearned to hurt Kilraven, to punch him and go on punching him until Kilraven was in a bloody heap at his feet.

Severn had stepped back, his rifle level. "Come along, now. Be a good Yank and you will make it home in one piece."

"You can go to hell, too."

Bromley started to reach out as if to place a hand on Simon's shoulder. But he stopped and said, "Please don't make this any more difficult than it has to be, Mr. Ward. I happen to like you and your wife, and would rather we can go on being sociable."

"You work for a monster," Simon said.

Severn indicated the buckboard. "That will be quite enough. No more insults. Climb in your wagon and we will escort you home."

Felicity gripped her husband's wrist. Peter was asleep on her shoulder, his face angelic in repose. "Please, Simon," she said. "Please."

"I am fit to explode," Simon said, but he relented. Hooking her arm in his, he headed for the buckboard.

They had only taken a couple of steps when Cadena was beside them. "Please don't hate us. Not everyone agrees with my uncle's methods."

"Does that include you?" Felicity asked.

"I would pay you more than he is willing to," Cadena said.

Simon looked at her. He just looked.

"What? It is not the same as stealing, is it, if you are paid for your property, and paid well? Maybe I can persuade him to add four or five hundred dollars to whatever amount you want. Extra compensation for all your effort."

"You don't seem to get it," Simon said. "The money is not important."

Cadena laughed. "Money is always important. Those who think otherwise are those who do not have any."

"You are as fond of it as he is," Felicity remarked.

"I like the finer things in life, yes," Cadena confessed. "And the finer things are not free. My uncle's venture here will considerably increase the family coffers. If you must be inconvenienced a bit, so be it."

Simon did not hide his disgust. "Go away."

"Mr. Ward, really."

"Leave us," Simon insisted.

"Very well. But I trust you will come to your senses. Perhaps you would like to have tea with us tomorrow?"

"I would rather dine with pigs than sit at your table again."

Cadena slowed and fell behind, saying, "You are one for theatrics, aren't you? But I will not take your abuse personally. We say a lot of things we do not mean in the heat of anger."

From that moment until the moment the dark silhouette of their cabin came into sight, Simon did not say another word. Molten lava boiled within him, and he was afraid if he did say something, he would bring the wrath of their escorts down on their heads.

The buckboard was fifty yards from the cabin when Severn drew rein and announced, "This is as far as we go. We bid you good night, Mr. and Mrs. Ward."

"Go to hell," Simon responded.

"Remember, we will have someone keeping an eye on you at all times," Bromley said. "Please behave yourselves and there will not be any trouble."

"You can go to hell, too."

Simon did not stop the buckboard until he was at their cabin. Jumping down, he reached up to assist his wife and son.

"Didn't we leave the lamp on?" Felicity asked.

Simon drew up short. Now that she mentioned it, they had. It had been her idea, so they would have light to see by when they got home. Puzzled, he turned and went to open the front door, but it swung inward of its own accord, and before he could so much as blink, a rifle muzzle was thrust in his face.

Chapter Six

Simon Ward's first thought was that Lord Kilraven had sent someone on ahead with the intent of killing them outright and taking their land. Then a chuckle broke the stillness.

"If I was a Piegan or a Blood, you would be pushing up daises come morning."

Recognition stunned Simon.

"Cat got your tongue?" Out stepped a handsome young man in buckskins. "Where in blazes have you folks been? I cut the trail of a war party on my way here and I was half afraid they had gotten hold of you and I would have to avenge you." He chuckled. "Not that I mind avenging."

Felicity found her tongue first. "Zach!" she blurted, and launched herself at him with Peter clasped tight at her side. "Oh, Zach!" She leaned against his chest, and for the second time that night struggled to fight down tears. "You are a godsend."

Zachary King looked from her to Simon and

back again. He was not as tall nor as broad as his father, but he was a strapping figure in his own right. His mother's Shoshone inheritance showed in his swarthy complexion and his long black hair, worn Shoshone fashion. Like his renowned sire, he was armed with a Hawken, a brace of pistols, a knife and a tomahawk. Moccasins, a possibles bag, and ammunition pouch and powder horn completed the rough-hewn portrait. "Is something the matter?"

Simon quickly took the younger man by the arm and pulled him into the cabin, whispering, "We must keep our voices down. You are not safe."

"We are in trouble," Felicity said. "Dire trouble."

"Do I get to shoot someone?" Zach asked, and his teeth shone white in the darkness.

"This is serious," Simon said, going to the door. He listened, but there was no indication Kilraven's men had heard. It might be they had all gone back to camp except for the watchdog.

"So am I," Zach said. If there was anything he liked more than counting coup, he had yet to come across it.

"Where is your horse?" Simon asked.

"In your corral. My pack animal, too. I thought I would stay the night and head for Bent's Fort in the morning."

"Is that where you are bound?" Felicity asked while carrying Peter to his bed in the corner. They did not have a separate bedroom for him yet. Simon had been meaning to add one, but there never seemed to be enough time.

"My pa sent me to buy supplies," Zach explained. "And Louisa wants me to get her some perfume, of all things."

"What is wrong with that?" Felicity tenderly tucked a blanket to Peter's chin. "Lou is your wife, after all."

"Buying perfume is for females to do," Zach complained. "It is not fitting for a man. Besides, she smells fine just as she is except on hot days. And I don't mind a little stink."

"Perfume smells better than stink," Felicity teased.

"What do you have against bear fat?" Zach rejoined, and grinned.

Simon closed and barred the door, then went to the window and drew the curtains. "Light the lamp, but keep it low."

Felicity hurried to the table. "It is a good thing Zach turned down the lamp to surprise us. Otherwise they might have seen him."

"Who are you talking about?" Zach rested the stock of his Hawken on the floor and leaned on the barrel. "What in blazes is going on? You two act spooked."

Together they told him. Felicity brewed coffee and they sat at the table and related every detail of their encounter with Lord Kilraven and the lord's party. When they were done they sat back and Simon asked, "What do you think we should do?"

Zach King had not expected anything like this. He thought maybe they were having trouble with the Utes, or possibly white cutthroats. Hostiles and badmen Zach knew how to deal with; he disposed of them, permanently, and that was that. A high English muck-a-muck was another matter. Disposing of him might bring the wrath of the federal government down on his head, and after the recent ordeal he went through after he wiped out a bunch of white traders who had tried to stir up a war between the Shoshones and the Crows, he would prefer to avoid another conflict with the United States military. He must be careful how he went about helping the Wards.

But help them Zach would. They had been friends of his family for years. Zach particularly liked that unlike most whites, they did not regard him as less than they were because he was a breed. They had always treated him exactly as they treated everyone else, and after all the abuse he had suffered at the hands of bigots, both white and red, he valued their special friendship that much more.

Now, shifting in his chair, Zach idly ran a finger around the edge of his coffee cup and commented, "We can't let this Kilraven get away with it."

"I couldn't agree more," Simon said. "But two of us is not enough."

"Three," Felicity said.

Simon leaned toward Zach. "We need your father and Shakespeare McNair. How long would it take you to bring them?"

"A week to ten days to reach the valley," Zach said. "A week to ten days to make the return trip."

"That long?" Simon asked, dismayed. "Kilraven only gave us four days to pack up and be ready to leave."

"I would like to meet this bastard," Zach said, and instantly glanced sheepishly at Felicity. "Sorry for the language."

"That's perfectly all right. I happen to think he's a bastard, too." Felicity grinned.

"Felicity!" Simon declared.

Zach snorted with mirth, then sobered. "My pa and Uncle Shakespeare could not make it back in time to be of any help. It's up to us."

Simon's despair climbed. He liked the younger King, liked him a lot, but Zach was not Nate. Zach did not have Nate's experience, Nate's wisdom. Zach was noted for his temper, not his sagacity. Plus one other thing: Zachary King was widely feared as a killer.

"But what can the three of us do against so many?" Felicity asked, nearly heartbroken. "We are no match for them."

"Not with guns and blades, we're not," Zach said. "But what if we beat them another way? What if we outthink them?"

"How is that again?" Simon asked.

"My pa likes to say there are three ways to best an enemy. One is to be stronger. The second way is to be quicker at drawing a pistol or stabbing with a knife. The third way, the way he likes best, is to outthink them, to be smarter than they are, to use the brain to do what a pistol or a knife or brute brawn cannot."

"Easier said than accomplished," Simon said. "Lord Kilraven strikes me as shrewd."

"Extremely shrewd," Felicity amended.

"Then we have to be shrewder." Zach tilted his

chair back on its rear legs and folded his arms. There had to be a way. His father was always fond of saying any problem could be solved if he thought about it long enough and hard enough. "You say this Kilraven wants to set up a hunting preserve? Is that what you called it?"

"Yes," Simon confirmed. "Then he will advertise in his country and in Europe, inviting those with money to burn to spend it at his lodge."

Felicity stirred. "Our valley is only a small part of the territory he's claiming. His preserve will stretch from the foothills into the mountains."

"This lord, is he familiar with the country hereabouts?" Zach asked.

"Not that we're aware," Simon said. "I had the impression that most of what he knows is hearsay."

"If that's so, then maybe we can use his ignorance against him," Zach proposed. The germ of an idea had taken root.

"You've lost me," Felicity said. "Unless you mean to ride to the Shoshones and ask their help."

"We can't involve them." Zach had gotten his mother's people into enough trouble. Most whites considered the Shoshones the friendliest tribe on the frontier and tended to treat them better than other tribes, and he wanted them to go on doing so.

Simon was excited by the prospect. "There is no need to spill blood. Have Touch the Clouds bring a hundred warriors and surround Kilraven's camp. I guarantee his lordship will fold his tents and skulk off with his tail between his legs."

"What if you misjudge him?" Zach said. "What if he decides to make a fight of it? Shoshones will be killed." He shook his head. "We cannot involve my mother's people."

"Then what do you have in mind?"

Zach swallowed coffee, smacked his lips, and grinned. "I'll keep that to myself for the time being, if you don't mind. What you don't know can't get you beat up."

Felicity stared at the small bed in the corner and bit her lower lip. "I'm scared, and I don't mind admitting it. We stand to lose everything we have worked so hard to build." She stifled a yawn.

"That won't happen," Zach assured her.

"I wish I had your confidence."

"I have my pa to thank. Since I was old enough to toddle, he was forever telling me that a King never gives up, never says die, never lets hardship stop us."

Simon smothered a yawn of his own. "I cannot tell you how much I admire your father." He was sincere. Few men ever impressed him as greatly as Nate King. Nate would do anything for a friend, anything at all, up to and including risking his life on their behalf, as he had done for them on several occasions. Simon loved the man as a brother.

"I say we all turn in and discuss this further in the morning," Felicity suggested.

"Fine by me," Zach said, standing. "I'll sleep out in the barn."

"You will do no such thing," Felicity said. "We have plenty of room and plenty of spare blankets. You'll sleep in here with us—no arguments."

"Careful, Zach," Simon quipped. "Get her dander up and she's a regular hellion."

Felicity rose. "I will not have any guest of ours

sleep in the hayloft when we have a perfectly comfortable floor."

The truth be known, Zach would rather sleep in the loft. Hay was soft, if prickly, and the scent always reminded him of clover. "Here will do, then." Another thing his father had taught him was that arguing with a woman was like arguing with a tree. It got a man nowhere.

Presently, Zach lay on his back with his head in his hand and gazed at the ceiling. He could not get to sleep. He could not stop thinking about the idea he had come up with, and the consequences.

A sound outside brought Zach up on his elbows. He strained his ears and heard it again, the stealthy tread of someone moving past the front of the cabin. He had Felicity to thank. She had opened the window a few inches to admit the night breeze.

The tread came to the front door and stopped. Zach's right hand crept to his tomahawk.

Over in the corner little Peter mumbled in his sleep. Simon and Felicity were in their bedroom.

Whoever was outside moved to the window. A silhouette bathed in moon glow played over the curtains.

Zach rose into a crouch. The Wards had mentioned that Kilraven left a man to watch them. Leaving his rifle on the blankets, Zach glided to the window. He heard the man breathing, heard a grunt, and then the shadow moved on. Zach parted the curtains and peeked out.

The man was walking off. All Zach saw was his back, but it was enough. Never taking his eyes off the man's head, Zach raised the window high enough to slip out. He was grateful when it did not catch or creak. Hiking his right leg, he slid over the sill. He had to bend to ease his body out, and then he was flat against the wall, his tomahawk in his right hand.

The guard still had no idea he was there, and was peering around the corner toward the back of the cabin.

Zach crept closer.

The man turned toward the barn and corral. He began to hum to himself, as if he did not have a care in the world.

Suddenly springing, Zach swept the flat of his tomahawk against the man's temple. Two blows proved to be enough. The man folded at the knees and pitched onto his chest and face.

"Easy as pie," Zach remarked, and hurriedly stripped the guard of a rifle, a pistol, and a knife. Removing the man's belt, Zach used it to bind his wrists behind his back. He cut strips from the man's coat and used those to bind his ankles.

Grabbing hold of the man's legs, Zach dragged him toward the stream and into a small stand of cottonwoods that grew on the near bank.

Something snorted, and a four-legged form flashed out of the trees, streaking past Zach in high bounds. He dropped a hand to his pistol, then realized what it was. "Stupid deer," he grumbled.

The stream was a silver ribbon that gurgled and hissed as if alive. Zach dragged the guard to the water's edge. Drawing his knife, he ran a finger along the edge, checking that it was sharp. Dull knives made for early graves. Bending, he dipped his other hand in the water. It was cold, even in the summer. Cupping some, he splashed it on the man's face.

Nothing happened.

Zach had to do it four times before the man sputtered and blinked and his eyes opened.

Holding the knife so the man could see the blade, Zach said in Shoshone, *"Tsaangu yeyeika, dosabite sadee'a."* Translated, it meant, 'Good evening, white dog.'

Then Zach pressed the edge to the man's throat.

Chapter Seven

"Cor!" the man shrieked. "The savages have me!"

Zach pressed hard enough to cut the skin but no deeper. A dark trickle formed.

"Bloody hell!" the man screeched, his eyes nearly bulging from their sockets. "Please! God! Don't kill me!" He started to shake in abject fear and gritted his teeth to keep them from chattering.

"*Su'ahaibeidee,*" Zach said in disgust. He gripped the man's hair as if intending to yank his head back.

"By all that's holy!" the man wailed. "I don't want to die! Do you understand?"

Zach pretended to pause.

The man was drenched with sweat. Licking his lips, he said in a terror-struck rush, "I don't speak your heathen tongue. Do you speak mine? Do you know English? If you do, if you know any at all, you must know what friend means. I am your friend. Do you understand? Friend!"

"Friend?" Zach repeated quizzically.

"Yes! Yes! By God, yes!" The man's mouth creased in a petrified smile and he bobbed his stubble-flecked chin. "I am a friend! I mean you no harm! No harm at all!"

Zach let go of the oily hair and slowly lowered his knife.

Tears welled in the man's eyes. He quaked more violently than before, only this time in profound relief. "Thank you, thank you, thank you! You won't regret this. I am your friend and I can prove it."

"Friend?" Zach said again.

"I am new to this country. You are the first bloody savage I have met." The man gulped at his own stupidity. "Sorry. I meant you are the first Indian I have met. Blimey! I don't even know what tribe you are."

Zach pressed his hand to his chest. "Me Blackfoot," he declared.

"My guts for garters! I have heard of your tribe." The man glanced wildly about for succor that was not there. "They say you are the worst of the lot. That you hate whites and kill every white man you come across."

"Straight tongue, white dog," Zach said. "We kill Wards. Now we kill you."

The man's relief had been short-lived. "Oh God, oh God, oh God! But I am your friend, I tell you! I have never done any of your people harm! Not ever! Why kill me?"

Zach extended his arm toward the flat-topped hill at the far end of the valley. "We see fires. We see many whites."

"Bloody hell." The man twisted and propped

himself on his forearms. "Listen. Please. Those I am with, they are your friends, too."

"All friends?" Zach said, struggling not to laugh.

"All of us, yes!" the man desperately averred. "I can prove it! Take me there, and the man I work for—what do you heathens call them again?—my chief, that's it, my chief, will reward you for sparing my life. Would you like that? A new blanket, maybe? Or an axe?"

Zach shammed mulling the offer over and had to look away when the man briefly forgot himself and smiled slyly at his ruse. It had been Zach's experience that there was no shortage of idiots in the world.

"What do you say, Blackfoot? Friends, yes? Cut me loose and I will take you there."

Bending down, Zach lightly jabbed the tip of his knife into the man's neck. "You lie, white scum."

"No! No! Honest I don't!" the man squealed.

"You lie," Zach went on. "All whites lie. My people hate white-eyes. My people kill every white." He raised the knife over his head as if for a fatal thrust. "Now I kill you."

To his amazement, the man shut his eyes and began shrilly praying. "The Lord is my shepherd, I shall not want. He maketh me to lie down in green pastures. He restoreth my soul—"

The man went on but Zach did not listen. He was remembering the evening ritual at the King cabin when he was a boy. Every night, without fail, his father read to him and his sister. It might be a short story by Washington Irving or Nathaniel Hawthorne. It might be *The Last of the Mohicans* by James Fenimore Cooper. One time it was Mary Shelley's *Frankenstein.* Or it might be excerpts from the Bible, especially Psalms, of which his father was especially fond. Zach gave his head a toss to clear it of memories and glanced down. His captive was finishing Psalm 23.

"—and I will dwell in the house of the Lord forever." The man cracked his eyelids and stared at the upraised knife. "Well? Are you or aren't you? I have made my peace. I am ready."

Zach let his arm drop to his side. "Maybe me not kill."

The man craned his neck and gazed skyward at the stars. "Thank you, God! I will never doubt my wife again."

"What be name?" Zach demanded.

"Owen. Reginald Owen."

Zach pointed to the west again. "You go other whites, Reginald Owen. Tell whites leave! Leave or Blackfeet kill!"

"Yes, yes, whatever you want."

"Leave or all die," Zach stressed. He had high hopes it would work. The Blackfoot Confederacy was widely feared, both by other tribes and whites alike. The rest of the Brits, like this one, were bound to have heard of them, and like as not would not want to tangle with a Blackfoot war party. Since reasoning with Lord Kilraven was out of the question, Zach had decided to try another tactic: fear.

"I will tell the man I work for," Owen was prattling. "I give you my word I will tell him. But what if he won't believe me? What if he refuses to leave?"

"All whites die," Zach growled. He motioned to encompass the cottonwoods and the surrounding prairie. "We have two hundred warriors. We attack camp. We kill and kill."

"Two hundred!" Owen bleated, and looked about him in terror. "Eight times our number!"

"You tell whites!" Zach commanded.

Owen nodded vigorously. "I will, I will, I give you my word. Trust me when I say none of us want to have our throats slit or our hair taken. Why the hair, anyway? What do you do with it?"

"You stupid man," Zach said.

"All right, all right. Forget I asked. I will tell the others. God willing, we will be gone just as fast as we can."

"Tomorrow by sinking of sun," Zach said. He was having fun with his deception, but he had to keep in mind what was at stake. The Wards were counting on him. He must not let them down.

"That soon? You won't give us a couple of days to rest up?" Owen said. "I don't know if his lordship will agree. We have tents to strike, packs to repack, that sort of thing."

Zach wagged the knife under his nose. "By time sun go down!"

"Sure, sure, whatever you want! Just be careful with that great bloody blade of yours."

"Straight tongue, white dog?"

Reginald Owen sat up. "As God is my witness. Do you think I want my friends massacred by your heathen breathren?"

"You tell them leave," Zach said. "Leave or ground

be red with blood." He was laying it on thick, as the whites liked to say, but the situation called for it. "Their blood."

"I said I would, haven't I?" Owen testily responded. "Come on. Cut me free and I will be on my way."

Zach sliced the cloth strips around his ankles first, then moved around behind him and cut the belt that bound his wrists.

Rubbing them, Owen rose to his knees. His pants, beltless, slid down around his feet. "What the hell?" he blurted. "Where did my belt get to?" He groped about, found a piece on the ground, and examined it to verify what it was. "Damn you. This was the only belt I own."

"Damn me, white man?" Zach said, and clubbed him with the hilt of the knife.

Owen swayed and clutched his head but was not knocked unconscious. He stared aghast at the blade Zach flourished before his eyes, bleating, "Sorry! I forgot myself."

"Where your horse?"

"I left it off there a ways," Owen said, gesturing vaguely westward.

"Take me," Zach commanded. Gripping the man's shoulder, he roughly hauled him erect, and shoved. "Walk quick." Zach jabbed him low in the back to speed him along.

"I'm going! I'm going!"

Inwardly, Zach smiled. He debated slicing off the man's nose or an ear. That was what a real Blackfoot warrior would do. The Blackfeet hated whites, ill will bred by the Lewis and Clark expedition. A clash between the explorers and the Blackfeet resulted in one Blackfoot being stabbed to death and another shot, a slight the Blackfeet had never forgotten. But mutilating Owen might enrage the British lord and his party and put them in a mood to fight. Zach wanted them to leave. He gave Owen another push.

"I'm doing the best I can, damn it," the man grumbled. "I'm not a bloody owl. I can't see in the dark."

The horse had been left with its reins dangling about a hundred and fifty yards from the Ward's cabin. Owen went to take hold of them, but Zach snatched them from his grasp.

"No. Me keep horse."

"What?" Owen gazed toward the far end of the valley, apprehension twisting his features into a mirror of fear. "You expect me to walk all that distance? At night?"

"We not harm you," Zach said. "You must tell other whites our words." He reminded himself to talk like someone who barely knew English.

"I will, I will. Only I can do it a lot faster if I ride."

"No." Zach needed to gain the Wards as much time as possible. It would take Owen hours to reach the camp on foot.

"But there are beasties abroad," Owen glumly protested. "I could be eaten."

As if to accent his plea, a faint roar echoed down from the timbered slopes high above. A grizzly was in a foul temper. Almost on its heels came the wavering howl of a roving wolf.

"No," Zach said again. The man was in very little danger. Simon Ward had long since cleared the valley of predators that might do his family harm. He pricked Owen in the ribs. "Go now."

Exhibiting great reluctance, the hapless Brit bent his steps into the darkness. He glanced back several times, apparently afraid it was all a trick and he would be slain anyway.

As soon as the night swallowed him, Zach made a rapid beeline for the cabin. He tied the horse to the corral rail and entered the cabin by the window. Once inside, he closed the window, then crossed the room.

Over in the corner Little Peter was breathing heavily, deep in sleep.

Zach pushed the bedroom door halfway open. "Simon! Felicity!" he whispered. "You need to get up and get dressed!" He went to the cast-iron stove and rekindled the embers. He was putting the coffeepot on to brew when the Wards emerged, yawning and rubbing their eyes but fully clothed.

"What is it?" Simon asked. "What's so urgent?"

Zach explained about the man left to watch them and what he had done. "I have convinced him you are dead and that the Blackfoot war party will wipe out the lord and his bunch if they don't light a shuck."

"It might work," Felicity said. "But Lord Kilraven strikes me as the kind who does not scare easily. What if he doesn't believe it? What if he comes here to see our bodies with his own eyes?"

"We will be long gone," Zach said. "I am taking you up into the high country where you will be safe." He had hunted the territory since he was old enough to ride and knew the region from the Green River to the Arkansas River as well as any man alive.

Simon gazed about the room. "Leave our home?"

He could imagine Kilraven ordering the cabin be burned to the ground, along with everything in it. They did not have a lot of furniture and possessions, but they could ill afford to lose the few they had.

"We must make it look as if the Blackfeet really did attack," Zach proposed. "Turn over the table and the chairs, throw some clothes around, kill one of your chickens and leave its blood all over the place."

"Have chicken blood all over my house?" Felicity envisioned the resultant mess, and how difficult it would be to clean up.

"We must make it look convincing. They will think the Blackfeet carried you off."

"I don't know," Simon said. He trusted Zach, and liked the idea of tricking Kilraven into leaving, but he would as soon cut off an arm as have everything he had worked so hard to build be destroyed.

"It's either that or make a stand here," Zach pointed out. "How many men did you say this lord has again?"

Simon turned to Felicity and clasped her hands in his. "I will leave it up to you. Do we or don't we? We could come back to find our home and our barn razed and all our animals dead."

Felicity gazed at their son, slumbering so peacefully and innocently. A lump formed in her throat. She loved their cabin. It was not much by Eastern standards, but she had worked hard to make it a home, and she would be devastated were they to lose it.

Simon intuited her feelings from her expression. Usually, in matters of importance, they both had a say in what they would do, but in this instance he wanted her to have the final word.

Swallowing hard, Felicity said softly, "I guess we have no choice. They took our guns so we can't fight them, and even if they hadn't, there are just too many of the scoundrels."

Simon faced Zach. "We will do as you suggest. Give us fifteen minutes to get ready."

"Take an hour," Zach said. "There is plenty of time. It will be morning before any of them can get here. That gives us most of the night to get you up into the mountains." Zach smiled. "Eat a meal. Pack your valuables. We will take whatever you want."

"What about our animals? The chickens and pigs and horses and our cow?"

"Everything except the horses can stay. The Blackfeet love to steal horses almost as much as they love to count coup on whites."

Felicity came to him and put her hand on his shoulder. "I can't tell you how much this means to us. And I must say, I'm surprised. Given how blood-thirsty people say you are, I am delighted at how hard you are trying not to spill blood."

Zach did not tell her that he was doing it for their benefit. "Let's hope this works. If it doesn't, the blood spilling will come later, and there will be a godawful lot of it."

Chapter Eight

Lord Laurence Kilraven hated America. He hated their salty, fatty food; in the mornings they ate toast drenched in butter with eggs and ham or beef smeared in hog's lard; in the evening it was more food drowning in lard and fat, and pastries and pies sickeningly rich in butter. He hated their clothes; they wore shabby homespun, for the most part, and well worn, at that, to the point where most of the population went about in the semblance of penniless ragamuffins. He hated their obsession with tobacco; they were constantly chewing and spitting, spitting and chewing. At the theater one evening in St. Louis, or what passed for a theater in America, a patron had the temerity to let loose with a wad of thoroughly masticated tobacco at his feet. He would have beaten the man senseless with his cane if he'd had his cane with him.

America did have one trait Lord Kilraven admired, the *only* trait he could say this about, namely:

their obsession with money. He shared that obsession. The Kilraven fortune had declined to the point where he was desperate to fill the family coffers. Hence his inspiration to open the first hunting preserve of its kind in all North America.

If there was one thing Lord Kilraven hated more than America, it was being rousted out of a sound sleep. He seldom slept well as it was, so to be blissfully asleep and then to hear his manservant, Caruthers, insistently if politely whispering his name, provoked a flush of anger. "What in God's name is it?" he demanded harshly.

"Begging your pardon, sir, but Mr. Severn is outside. He says he must speak to you. It is most urgent." Caruthers was fully dressed. He was required to be at Kilraven's beck and call, day and night, and slept on a cot near the front of the tent.

Kilraven was loathe to rise but did so. He sat up in bed—a bed, not a cot, he would not deign to sleep on a cot—then stood and shrugged into the robe Caruthers held for him. He glanced at his snoring wife and frowned. "Remind me again why I married her?"

"Sir?"

"Nothing." Kilraven strode to the front of their tent and pushed on the flap and stepped out into the chill late night hair. Half the camp had been aroused and many of the men had gathered, some, to his annoyance, in various stages of undress. "Well? This had better be important."

"I am sorry to disturb you, your lordship," Severn said. "But Owen has just shown up, and he bears bad tidings."

It took Kilraven a few seconds to recall that Owen was the man assigned to watch the Ward cabin. "Where is he?"

Severn moved aside.

Reginald Owen was a mess. He was caked with sweat. His shirt was half-out and he was holding his beltless pants up with one hand. The bottom of his pants and his shoes were brown with dust. Red in the face, he was partly bent over, his body quaking as he gasped for breath.

"What happened to you?"

"I am about done in, sir," Owen wheezed. "I ran most of the way, never knowing when those heathens might change their minds and put an arrow in my back."

"Explain yourself," Kilraven instructed him, and listened impatiently while his sputtering underling narrated his harrowing experience. When Owen finally finished, Kilraven thoughtfully rubbed his chin. "You say these Blackfeet will wipe us out if we don't leave?"

"The red bugger's very words, sir," Owen confirmed.

Kilraven had hoped to avoid clashes with savages. He had brought trinkets to give them and gain their goodwill in the event his party encountered any. The Blackfeet, though, were supposed to despise whites so much that trading with them was out of the question. "You went up to the Ward cabin at one point, did you not?"

"That I did, sir," Owen answered. "Mr. Severn ordered me to keep a close watch and warned they might try to sneak off."

"Did you then, or at any other time, hear anything that would lead you to conclude they were murdered by the heathens?"

"I did not, sir. It was as quiet as could be. The first I knew those devils were there was when I came to after being hit on the head."

"You heard no outcries? No indications of a struggle? Nothing of that nature?"

"No, sir."

"And how many Blackfeet did you see? Be exact."

"Just the one, sir."

"Only the one?" Lord Kilraven ran a hand through his shock of white hair. "There is something queer here. Mr. Severn, I want to talk to our scout, as he calls himself. Where is he?"

"The last I saw, under one of the wagons, sound asleep."

"Fetch him, and be quick about it. I will be back out." Kilraven went into the tent and had Caruthers help him dress.

"Should I wake Lady Kilraven, sir?"

"Whatever for?" Kilraven snapped. "I endure her useless prattle enough as it is. Let her sleep."

"As you wish, sir."

By the time Lord Kilraven reemerged, everyone was on hand except his wife and his niece. At the forefront stood a lanky man in dirty buckskins, his stringy brown hair poking from under a floppy brown hat. He had a bony forehead and bony cheeks, and a jagged ridge of scar tissue where his left ear should be. A Hawken was cradled in the crook of his right elbow. At his waist were two flintlocks and a bone-handled knife. He was chewing tobacco, but he stopped to say, "You sent for me, your highness?"

Lord Kilraven drew himself up to his full height. "How many times have I told you not to address me at that, Mr. Ryker? I am not the king of England. I am a baron."

"I don't know barons from bear skite," Ryker responded with more than a trace of insolence.

Severn took immediate offense. "You will address his lordship with the respect his title deserves."

Ryker spat a wad of tobacco, and smirked. "I will talk any damn way I please, mister, and if you don't like it, you're welcome to try and do something about it."

Kilraven held up a hand, silencing the reply Servern was about to make. "Stop this petty bickering. A situation has developed, Mr. Ryker, and I need your expert opinion."

"Is that so?" Ryker opened his possibles bag and took out a pouch. He undid the tie string, dipped his fingers inside, and stuffed a large pinch of a reddish substance into his mouth.

"More tobacco," Lord Kilraven said in undisguised disgust.

"Hell no, your highness," Ryker responded. "Tobacco can't hold a lick to this. It is kinnikkinnik."

Despite himself, Kilraven was curious. "That sounds Indian to me."

"It is," Ryker said. "Kinnikkinnik is made from willow bark. The red willow, not the other. You chew it like tobacco, but it tastes and smells better."

He closed the pouch and slid it back into his possible bag. "Chew enough of it and you feel like you can walk on water."

"Are you saying it is a narcotic?"

"I'm saying you feel real good. If that's what narcotic means, then yes." Ryker chewed lustily. "Now what's this all about? Someone mentioned the Blackfeet."

Lord Kilraven explained and had Reginald Owen repeat his account of his run-in with the Blackfoot warrior. Ryker listened without interrupting until Owen came to the part where the warrior had led him to his horse.

"Hold on, hoss. That's enough. I agree with his highness, here. Something doesn't add up." Ryker spat kinnikkinnik juice. "Describe this Blackfoot for me? Was he wearing war paint? What weapons did he have? What were his moccasins like? Give me all the details you can."

Owen obliged, and when he was done, Ryker indulged in a hearty chuckle. "I'll be damned."

"What is it?" Lord Kilraven asked, and was peeved when the American ignored him and instead addressed Owen.

"You mentioned that you heard this so-called Blackfoot speak Injun? Can you remember what he said?"

"Not very well, I am afraid," Owen replied. "It was something like *sue had dee.*"

"Could it have been *su'ahaibeidee*?"

Owen nodded enthusiastically. "It very well could have been, yes. What does it mean? Was it a threat?"

Ryker laughed. "He was saying you are an idiot,

and I agree." Ryker turned to Lord Kilraven. "That there is Shoshone, not Blackfoot. My hunch was right. That was no Injun. It was Zach King."

"King? That name is familiar. Where have I heard it before?"

"From me, at Bent's Fort, when you hired me," Ryker said. "I warned you about Zach's pa, Nate. Remember? Warned you about how the Kings and the Wards are good friends and how Nate King won't stand for having his friends driven from their homestead."

"Ah, yes, the mountain man," Kilraven said. "He is the reason you refused to stay with the wagons when we came up the valley. Instead, you went around and waited for us here."

"It's like I told you at Bent's Fort. The Wards are well thought of hereabouts. Folks won't take kindly to what you intend to do to them, and I don't want to be blamed for having a hand in it."

"All you are doing is serving as our guide," Kilraven said. "You cannot be held to account for my actions."

"Like hell I can't. Folks in this country take that kind of thing real personal. If their friends find out I guided you here, I could have cold steel stuck in my gizzard. That's why I don't want anyone, including the Wards, to know I am involved."

Lord Kilraven was sure the man was unduly concerned. But it was Ryker's problem, not his, and he would not waste another word on it. "Be that as it may, what about this boy, this Zach King?"

"He's no sprout, your highness. He's full growed, and in some respects, scarier than his pa."

"Scary how?" Again Kilraven thought the American was exaggerating.

"I know them both. I've never been to their cabins for supper, but I have talked to them a few times. Nate King is as highly regarded as Jim Bridger and Kit Carson. Those names might not mean much to you, but they carry a lot of respect on the frontier."

"It is the son who is the issue," Kilraven reminded him.

"I'll get to him in a minute," Ryker said. "Nate King is as honest as the year is long. He's loyal to his friends and fierce to his enemies. He's killed when he's had to, but only when he has to. He's not one of those who kills because he likes it. He's not like his son."

"What are you saying?"

"Aren't you listening? Zach King is half-Shoshone. The Shoshones are a peaceable tribe, but Zach's not peaceable. He likes to count coup. He's a warrior more than anything else. His pa will avoid bloodshed if he can help it, but the son goes straight for the throat. If he's helping the Wards, you're in for a fight."

"He is but one man," Kilraven scoffed. "He has no chance against our guns."

"Don't underestimate him," Ryker warned. "He's canny, that one. Clever as clever can be. His Injun name is Stalking Coyote, but it might as well be Stalking Fox."

"How quaint," Kilraven said with undisguised scorn.

Ryker frowned. "Suit yourself, you damned know-it-all. You hired me to guide you and give you my advice, and I'll give it now. You won't take it, but it's what you are paying me for." He paused. "Find somewhere else to build this preserve of yours. Don't try to force the Wards off their land or there will be hell to pay."

"I think you are right," Kilraven said.

Ryker blinked in surprise. "You do?"

"Yes. My original idea of having them escorted to Bent's Fort was based on the belief no one would dare lift a hand against me. But now you have convinced me otherwise. Now I must see to it that they do not reach Bent's Fort."

"You can't mean what I think you mean."

"There are two ways to resolve a dispute, Mr. Ryker. One is to sit down with the other party and talk things out. That will not work in this case. The Wards refuse to sell. The second way is to get rid of those who oppose you. I now intend to eliminate the Wards, and this Zach King if he stands in my way."

"By eliminate you mean kill?"

"Do you have a problem with that, Mr. Ryker?"

"Damned right I do. There was no mention of killing when you hired me. You said you were forcing the Wards off their land, and that was it."

Kilraven spread his hands in front of him. "The situation has changed. I must adapt. I suggest you adapt, as well."

Ryker shook his head. "I won't be a party to killing."

"It is not as if you have not killed before. I asked around about you before I hired you. Discreetly, of course. You say this Zach King has a bit of a reputation. So do you. You have killed a score of men yourself, rumor has it. Most of them Indians, but not all. You can be fierce in your own right." Kilraven had found that flattery was an essential tool in persuading others to go along with his wishes. That, and one other thing. "But I respect your qualms. Would five thousand dollars over and above what I am paying you erase them?"

"Five thousand," Ryker repeated, stunned. "That's more money than I've ever had at any one time in all my born days."

"I have your cooperation, then? Before you answer, permit me to make the conditions perfectly clear. For that amount of money you will not function strictly as my guide. You are to take an active hand in disposing of the Wards and this Zach King. Not only will you hunt them down for me, but you will slay them yourself if afforded the opportunity. Understood?"

"Five thousand," Ryker said yet again, and grinned a grin of pure greed. "Mister, you have yourself a deal. Zach King and the Wards are as good as dead."

Chapter Nine

Zach led the Wards due south from their cabin. They crossed the valley floor and wound into the foothills. A mile in, Zach reined to the west, making for the mountains. He held the horses to a walk. They had a long ride ahead, and it would not be wise to unnecessarily tire them.

The foothills at night were dark and foreboding. Wooded tracts alternated with open ground. An occasional bluff broke the rolling terrain. Out of the northwest blew a stiff wind, bringing with it a cacophony of animal sounds; the grunts and roars of grizzlies, the howls of wolves, the yips of coyotes, and now and again the piercing shriek of a mountain lion, a screech so inhuman as to make the skin crawl.

To Zach the bestial racket was as ordinary as water. He was at home in the wild, and those were the wild's normal sounds. He had heard them nearly every night of his life. They had no more effect on him than distant yells and pistol shots in a city would have on a lifelong city dweller.

Not so Simon Ward. He could never get used to the bedlam at night. Every roar, every howl, every shriek, rubbed his nose in the fact that the nighttime was when the meat eaters were abroad. Predators ruled the darkness, and woe to the hapless plant eater, or human, who disregarded their reign. Even the Indians did not like to be out and about after the sun went down, a sentiment Simon fully shared.

Many a night Simon had sat in his cabin and listened to the riot of cries and been grateful he had sturdy walls between his family and the source of those cries.

Now there were no walls. Now they were heading up into the heart of the realm the beasts ruled, and his own heart beat faster as Simon contemplated the possible consequences to his loved ones. It compelled him to gig his mount and lead Dancer and the pack horses past Felicity, who was holding Peter on the saddle in front of her, so he could ride beside Zach.

"I have been thinking."

"Oh?"

"Maybe we should head down instead of up," Simon said. "We would be safe at Bent's Fort."

"There is a lot of open ground between your valley and the trading post. With your wife and the boy along, you would never reach it."

Simon opened his mouth to argue and closed it again. Zach was right. He slowed so his wife could come alongside him. "How are you holding up?"

Felicity was tired, and hungry, and anxious to her

core, but she smiled and said, "Fine as can be. I heard what you asked Zach, and I agree with him. Kilraven will never find us up in the high timber."

"Just so we don't come back to find our cabin burned to the ground," Simon said, expressing his innermost worry.

"If we do, we'll rebuild. With an extra room for Peter."

Simon glanced at their son. The boy was sound asleep, slumped against his mother. In his innocence, he did not appreciate the gravity of their plight. "Oh, to be that young again," Simon said wistfully.

"Not me," Felicity said. "I like being as I am."

"You would rather be a woman than a girl? Rather have all the worries of an adult instead of the carefree and happy existence of a child?"

"I'm happier being your wife than I have ever been. As for cares, we have them at every age, only they seem less than they were when we look back at them."

"I suppose."

A rumbling snort from out of the brush startled them. Simon raised his rifle to his shoulder.

"It was only a buck," Zach said over a shoulder.

"I hate this," Simon said in almost a whisper so only his wife heard. "I jump at every sound and shadow."

"The night takes some getting used to," Zach said. "When I was your son's age, I was the same as you."

"Good ears, young master King," Simon responded. "How is it you can hear so well?"

"Necessity, my pa would say," Zach replied.

"When you grow up in the wilderness, you learn to use your ears and your eyes and your other senses, or you die." He shifted in the saddle. They were southwest of the flat-topped hill, and approximately a thousand feet higher. The campfires sparkled like red jewels. By now Reginald Owen had reached the camp and told his tale.

Zach wished he could see Kilraven's face when he saw the overturned furniture and the chicken blood. That was a nice touch, the blood, Zach thought. It should convince his lordship to light a shuck for healthier climes.

To the north, a wolf raised its plaintive wail and was mimicked by a kindred lupine spirit to the west.

Zach breathed deep of the brisk air and smiled. He loved the wild haunts, loved the mountains and the plains. His visits back East had shown him that civilization was not for him. He could no more stand living in a town or city than he could living in a cage. Civilized men liked to hem themselves in with walls and buildings. But not Zach. Give him the wide open spaces. Give him endless forest and endless grass, and the freedom to roam as he willed.

Zach would never understand the attitude of his father's people. Why did they live like bees or ants? How was it they did not mind being told how they should live? It was bewildering. His father was not like that. His father dared to live according to his own ideals and not those imposed on him by politicians and the like. Zach respected his father for that, respected him highly. He was glad his father had raised him in the wilderness and not back East. He would suffocate there. He would expire for a lack of freedom.

Zach never gave being free a lot of thought until recently, when the army took him into custody and he was placed on trial for killings that had been perfectly justified. Being thrown behind bars did wonders for a man's perspective. To have his freedom denied had taught him, as no other lesson could, how exquisitely precious that freedom was.

Zach would never go East again if he could help it. He'd had his fill of civilized ways. Until the day the maggots fed on his putrefied flesh, he would stay west of the Mississippi River, where a man could do as he pleased and not answer to anyone or anything other than his own desires and his own conscience.

A feral hiss rose from a thicket ahead, but Zach did not stop. "It's only a bobcat," he said for the benefit of the Wards.

Felicity had involuntarily tensed at the sound and clutched Peter tighter to her. Relaxing, she gave thanks Zach had shown up. She did not like to think of the dire straits they would be in without his help. He was not his father, but she trusted him. Other homesteaders were wary of Zach, if not outright afraid of him, but not her. Yes, he had, by all accounts, spilled more than his share of blood, but he had a lot of his father in him, more, maybe, than he was willing to admit.

Out of the corner of her eye, Felicity regarded Simon. She loved him dearly, loved him more than she had ever loved anyone. He was a devoted husband

and father, and a fine provider. But there were times, and this was one of them, when she wished he were a bit more like Nate and Zach. Especially Zach. When she wished he were tougher, wished he were—dare she think it?—meaner. That was what it took to stand up to the Kilravens of the world: meanness. Turning the other cheek to men like Kilraven was asking to have it slapped.

Felicity would never tell Simon how she felt. He could never change, anyway. People had to be true to their nature, and it was her husband's nature to be kind and considerate and, above all, reasonable.

A loud crash in the woods to their left, attended by a series of guttural growls, brought them to a stop.

"What is it?" Simon asked, jerking his rifle up again. "Another deer?"

"A bear," Zach said.

Simon swiveled in the saddle, the better to protect his wife and son should it come charging out at them.

"A black bear," Zach elaborated. "It's skulking off."

Straining his ears for all he was worth, Simon, for the life of him, could only hear the wind in the trees. "How can you be sure it was a black bear and not a grizzly?"

"Silvertips don't mutter to themselves like blacks do," Zach replied. "When they growl, they mean business."

Simon would never have described the growling he heard as muttering, but he took Zach's word for it. The mountains were Zach's element, the habits of their four-legged inhabitants as well-known to him as his own. "You still haven't said where exactly you propose to take us?"

Zach gazed into the inky murk above. "Up yonder a ways. The lord and his bunch will never find you. You can rest, catch up on your sleep if you want, while I pay their camp a visit."

"You're going back down? Whatever for? What do you hope to accomplish?"

"To teach them that the wilderness is no place for those who like to eat at a fancy table and be waited on hand and foot."

Zach skirted a log. Obstacles were common, and he had to stay alert. He could tell the Wards were nervous, especially Simon. They clearly weren't used to nighttime treks.

The slope grew steeper. Zach angled to the right, where the going was easier. The ground was hard but not so hard they could avoid leaving tracks. A frontiersman would have no problem trailing them, but Simon had assured him that Lord Kilraven's party was composed entirely of Brits. Greenhorns, who couldn't track a buffalo across a mud wallow.

He had nothing to worry about from them.

Lord Kilraven stood in the doorway of the Ward cabin, his hands clasped behind his back, and surveyed the shambles. "You are positive savages were not responsible? Despite all the blood everywhere?"

Ryker was moving about the room, stepping over articles of clothing and kitchen utensils scattered willy-nilly. "Do you see any broken dishes? No. Is any of the furniture busted? No. Are the curtains torn to pieces? There they hang. Were the kitchen knives taken? No, there's one on the floor near your foot." Ryker chuckled. "This is Zach King's doing.

He made it appear real enough that you would think Injuns were to blame. But it doesn't fool me."

"Where did they go? That is the question," Kilraven said.

Ryker took the lit lamp Bromley was holding. "Let's go back out and have a look-see."

Ten men were with them, the rest left to safeguard the women and the camp. Only Severn had been permitted to dismount. The rest awaited orders, their rifles across their saddles.

"Do you want us to help him look about, your lordship?" Bromley asked Kilraven.

Ryker glanced at him. "If I needed help, mister, I'd say so. I am the tracker here, not you."

"I only wanted to be of service," Bromley explained.

Lord Kilraven intervened. "I will let you know when you can be." Of all those who worked for him, Kilraven liked Bromley the least. Not because Bromley was incompetent or impertinent. Far from it. He disliked Bromley because the man was too nice. Bromley avoided giving offense wherever possible, which was no way to make one's mark in the world.

Ryker cast about for prints. Bent low, the lamp in front of him, he roved in a wide arc around the cabin. "Over here," he called out, and sank to one knee. "See these?" He indicated where the ground was churned by heavy hooves.

"What of it?" Lord Kilraven said. "They are no different than any of the other tracks."

"These are fresh, your highness," Ryker said. "See this clod? How the dirt breaks apart when I touch it?

And this grass? How the stems are bent but slowly rising back up?" Ryker swung the lamp. "King, the Wards, and every last horse the Wards own, headed south. They want you to think the Blackfeet took them, but I know better."

"How much of a head start would you say they have?" Lord Kilraven inquired.

"Not enough," Ryker said. "At first light I'll head out. I should catch up to them by noon."

"Why not take torches and head out now?" Kilraven was impatient to get it over with, to dispose of the Wards and their friend so he could get on with establishing his hunting preserve.

"Because Zach King will see the torches and know a tracker is after him," Ryker answered. "It is smarter to take a hellion like him by surprise."

"Very well. First light it is. Take Mr. Meldon and four others, and don't let me see your faces again until you have done as I am paying you to do."

"I can make better time by my lonesome," Ryker mentioned.

"I imagine you can," Kilraven said. "But you will take my men with you anyway. They will not slow you down all that much." And he wanted someone along whose word on the outcome would be the un-varnished truth.

As if Ryker had read his mind, he angrily asked, "Don't you trust me to get the job done?"

"I trust no one," Lord Kilraven said. "Not even my wife. I have found that I suffer far fewer disappointments that way."

"I reckon I can't blame you there. Females are the

least trustworthy critters on God's green earth. But you can count on me. For five thousand dollars I'd plant my own brother."

"You are a man of few scruples," Lord Kilraven commented.

"You have a problem with that?" Ryker asked.

"On the contrary. I applaud you. I have marvelously few scruples myself. They are vastly overrated."

Ryker laughed. "I like your attitude, your highness. All right. I'll take some of your bootlickers along. But they're to do as I say."

"You heard, Mr. Bromley?"

"Yes, your lordship."

Kilraven gazed toward the foothills and the inky slopes above. "Find them, Ryker. Find them and eliminate them. If you make them suffer before they die for the inconvenience they have caused me, so much the better."

Chapter Ten

The mouth of the canyon was hidden by thick pines that fringed both sides. Unless someone knew of it, a person could pass within fifty feet and not realize it was there.

As Zach King led the Wards into the narrow opening, high rock walls rose on either side, blotting out much of the star-filled sky. The wind howled down the defile, a demented banshee that drowned out the dull thud of hooves. But the effect was temporary. Around the first bend the canyon widened to a quarter of a mile, and the wind was not as strong.

A few hundred yards in were thick woods and a spring. Zach had discovered the spot while on an elk hunt years ago with Shoshone friends. Or rather, Drags the Rope had discovered it when following elk tracks and brought Zach and the others.

Zach threaded through the firs and reined to a halt. "This is where you will wait."

Simon Ward had no idea where they were. They had been heading generally west, that much he knew, but he could not say exactly how far they had come nor how high up they were. Dawn was only a couple of hours away, he believed, if that. Stiffly dismounting, he held up his arms to Felicity so he could take Peter and she could dismount. "How are you holding up?"

"Just fine," Felicity fibbed. She was sore from so much riding and weary to her core. She also had a pain in her hip from holding Peter there for so long, a pain she could not relieve no matter how she shifted her weight or shifted him.

The boy was sound asleep.

Simon rested his son's cheek on his shoulder and carried him to the spring. "Can we have a fire?"

"It should be safe enough," Zach said. The high canyon walls would hide it from scrutiny from below. He roved among the firs, gathering downed limbs. Returning, he took a fire steel and flint from his possibles bag, as well as a small wooden box that contained tinder. Soon flames crackled and leaped.

Felicity prepared a bed for Peter. She folded several blankets and set them one atop the other. Simon tenderly laid the boy down, and together they covered him with another blanket, leaving only his head exposed. He stirred once and mumbled and then went back to sleep.

"To be so young and innocent," Simon said.

"You are still an innocent," Felicity said. "It is part of the reason I married you."

This was news to Simon. "A grown man can hardly be called innocent."

"In your heart you are," Felicity said. "You are good and decent, two qualities that go hand in hand with innocence."

Simon was disposed to debate the point, but just then Zach swung onto his horse. "You're off already?"

"I want to reach their camp before daylight," Zach said. It would take hard riding.

"Can't you rest a little?" Felicity urged. "By the time you get there, you will have been up all night."

"The sooner this is over, the sooner you can get on with your lives," Zack's replied. He gave them his final instructions. "Stay in the canyon. Keep the fire small. The only Indians that know of this spring, so far as I know, are the Shoshones, and this time of year they're up in the Green River country. This is Ute territory so there is always the chance some Ute might happen by."

"We're on good terms with them," Simon mentioned.

"Even so, mention my pa's name. He's a friend of theirs. Like as not they won't harm you."

Simon glanced at the high walls and his mouth went dry.

"Animals are another matter. Deer and such will stay away because of the fire, but a fire doesn't always scare off a griz. If you hear a bear, make the fire bigger and make a lot of noise. Whatever you do, don't shoot it unless you can see it and make sure you hit its vitals." Grizzlies were notoriously hard to kill. Zach had heard of instances where a griz was shot fourteen or fifteen times and still would not go down.

Felicity gazed at their sleeping son and fought down a surge of anxiety. "Don't worry about us, Zach. We'll be fine."

"How can I help but worry? You're my friends." Zach grinned, then jabbed his heels against his sorrel and rode down out of the canyon. The Wards were competent enough, but he did not like leaving them alone.

In order to get back to them that much sooner, Zach rode faster than he normally would. He was taking a risk. Fallen trees and other obstacles abounded, and should the sorrel break a leg, calamity loomed. But he stayed alert, and the sorrel was as sure-footed as always, and half an hour before sunrise found him warily climbing the boulder-strewn west slope of the flat-topped hill. Above, the glow from the campfires that had burned all night gave the illusion dawn was breaking.

Well below the crest Zach drew rein and slid down. No trees were handy, so he used a picket pin, a wooden stake he had whittled from a pine branch, to ensure the sorrel did not wander off. Then he stalked higher.

The whites were remarkably careless. Instead of patrolling the rim, as they should be doing, the sentries were closer to camp, one near the horse string, another to the south but standing near a fire, a perfect target.

Zach was tempted to run off their horses and whittle them down one by one. But he was not out to wipe them out. He wanted to drive them off. His idea was to kill a few and then give voice to war whoops and make enough other noise racket to convince them a large war party had descended on their camp. Odds were, they would flee back to the wretched civilization that spawned them.

Zach counted four females: an older woman in a flowing dress, the lord's wife, he figured; two women in uniforms whom he took to be servants; and a young girl, no more than sixteen and quite pretty. The niece, Simon had told him. A china cup and saucer were in her lap, and she was delicately sipping, as if she were having tea on a city terrace instead of in the dark heart of the wilderness.

Zach would not harm the women. He did not count coup on females. He watched them for a few minutes, particularly the young one; then he flattened and crawled to where he had a clear shot at the sentry who was warming his backside.

Zach felt no qualms as he wedged his Hawken to his shoulder. These people were invaders. They had waltzed in out of nowhere and were trying to force the Wards from the farm they had spent years building. That Lord Kilraven was in charge was a meaningless distinction. The others were either related to him or worked for him and were there to do his bidding, which made them as much to blame as their lord and master.

Still, the instant before he squeezed trigger, Zach shifted the bead a hair so he shot the sentry in the shoulder and not squarely in the chest. The impact of the heavy-caliber slug spun the man halfway around. Simultaneously, Zach let out with war whoops a Comanche would envy. Then, whirling, he bounded down the slope to the sorrel. He yanked out the pin, vaulted into the saddle, and galloped toward the bottom, expecting at any moment for rifles to boom and lead to whistle past his ears. But no shots rang out.

At the base of the hill, Zach reined to the right and raced around it until he was directly below the tents. He rode halfway up, dismounted again, and cat-footed to the top. No one was anywhere near. He could not see what was going on on the other side, but from the shouts and the sounds of men scurrying, he had some idea.

One of the tents was aglow with the light of a lantern. Running over, Zach drew his knife and thrust the tip into the canvas at shoulder height. He cut a slit down to about his ankles, and peered in. The tent was empty. A bed was on one side, a small dresser on the other. He grinned at the sight. They sure loved their creature comforts.

The lamp on the dresser interested Zach more. Slipping inside, he picked it up and raised it overhead. He was about to dash it on the bed when the front flap parted and in walked the pretty young girl.

Edwin Ryker was uneasy. He had agreed to track down Zach King and the Wards for five thousand dollars, and five thousand was a lot of money. But it would be of no use to him if he were dead, and tangling with the likes of Zach King was a surefire invite to an early grave.

Ryker had never liked Zach much. Part of his dislike had to do with the high regard in which the Kings were held. Nearly everyone—from the Bent brothers and St. Vrain at the trading post, to the mountain men who roamed the high country, to the friendly tribes of the mountains and the prairie—had the highest esteem for Nate King and his family. A much higher esteem, Ryker reflected, than they ever showed for him.

Another part of his dislike had to do with the fact Zach King was a half-breed. Ryker did not care for breeds, and he was not alone. They were widely looked down on. A lot of folks believed that mixing white blood and red blood tainted the offspring. Breeds were notorious for being hot tempered and violent. And while Ryker knew more than a few who were as peaceable as anyone else, he believed as the majority did, that breeds were bad medicine.

Which brought Ryker to the third reason he disliked Zach King. Zach had gone and married a white woman. A sweet gal Ryker had seen a couple of times at Bent's Fort, but a gal with no more brains than a turnip. Not if she wed a breed. Especially not when the breed was a confirmed man killer.

A lot of frontiersman killed. That was nothing new. Most had to at one time or another in order to preserve their lives. But Zach King was different. He had made wolf meat of more enemies—or counted more coup, as the redskins liked to say—than anyone. Or so gossip had it, and where breeds were concerned, Ryker was willing to believe whatever was said about them.

Ryker had plenty of reasons to want to plant Zach King and plenty of reasons to go about it in a way that ensured he would live to spend the money Kilraven was paying him.

Not that Ryker liked his high-and-mighty lordship any better than he liked Zach. Kilraven was puffed up with self-importance and went around bossing others as if it were his God-given right. Men like that deserved to be taught some humility.

All this and more filtered through Ryker's mind as he sat by a small fire near the Ward cabin, sipping coffee and waiting for daylight. The men Kilraven had left with him were asleep, all except Meldon, who sat across the fire, nipping from a flask.

"What do you have in there? Whiskey?"

"Bitters," the Brit said.

Ryker gazed to the east. It would not be long. A faint hint of gray marked the black vault. He sipped more coffee and caught Meldon staring at him. "What?"

"I was just wondering why you live as you do."

"I don't live any different than you," Ryker responded.

"How can you say that? You wear animal skins. You shoot, butcher, and eat your own meat. You roam land infested with savages and wild animals." Meldon shook his head. "You most definitely do live different than I do, governor. I buy my clothes from a shop in Liverpool. I like to eat at a pub. And the only savages I have to deal with are my seven kids."

"A man does what he has to," Ryker said.

"There has to be more to it than that," Meldon persisted. "Most people like to go to bed at night knowing they will still be alive to go to bed the night after."

"What can I tell you?" Ryker rejoined. "You like what you like, and I like what I like."

"You are a far braver bloke than I am, Yank. Me, I

want to enjoy old age, and rock in a rocking chair with a grandkid on my knee."

"Old age has never interested me," Ryker said. "Hobbling around on a cane is not my idea of living."

"When you get yourself a wife and kids, you won't think that way," Meldon commented.

Ryker thought of Zach King's wife and grew warm with anger. Casting the coffee in his cup to the ground, he stood. "Wake your pards. We're heading out."

"But the sun isn't up yet," Meldon noted.

"So what? You're to do as I say, and I say wake them." Ryker slid his tin cup into a parfleche and tied the parfleche to his horse. He checked his rifle and his pistols, then had to mentally twiddle his thumbs for fifteen minutes while the Brits prepared to head out. "Took you long enough," he grumbled when Meldon announced they were ready.

Ryker knew that Zach King had led the Wards south. He figured they would turn west and swing around the far end of the valley, and he was right, as the tracks revealed by the predawn light proved.

"Have you any idea where they are heading?" Meldon inquired as Ryker swung back on his mount.

"Maybe they have a hankering to throw snowballs at one another."

"Sorry?"

"Zach King will take them somewhere he thinks is safe," Ryker said. Somewhere up in the heavy timber, he imagined, gigging his horse parallel with the tracks. The trail was as plain as plain could be, and that troubled him until he realized Zach had no reason to expect a tracker was after them. If it went on like this, he would catch up in no time. The five thousand dollars was as good as his. He smiled, thinking of the many splendid ways he could spend it.

The sky was rapidly brightening. Soon dawn would break and the sun would rise.

"Mr. Ryker, sir!" Meldon suddenly exclaimed.

Ryker glanced sharply around. "What?"

"There! Look there!" Meldon pointed to the northwest. "Is that what I think it is?"

"Dear God!" one of the other men cried out.

Ryker could not resist an oath. A huge bonfire appeared to have been lit on top of the flat-crowned hill.

But it was no bonfire.

The tents were burning.

Chapter Eleven

Zach reacted in the blink of an eye. He assumed the girl would scream, and if she did, he'd be up to his neck in Brits. Accordingly, the instant she looked up and saw him, he was on her. He had the lamp in one hand and his Hawken in the other so he did the only thing he could; he jammed the muzzle against her side and warned, "So much as let out a peep and you'll be sorry." In the next heartbeat he hurled the lamp at the bed.

The girl's manicured hand flew to her throat, but she did not scream. Her eyes widened as flames flared on her bedspread. Crackling and multiplying with remarkable swiftness, they spread like a miniature wildfire.

"My quilt!" the girl squeaked.

"Didn't you hear me?" Zach gruffly demanded, gouging the barrel harder. "I said not a peep."

Apparently she did not take him seriously, or did

not care. "You brute! You terrible heathen brute! My grandmother gave me that quilt."

"How nice for you," Zach said, and grabbed her wrist. "You can tell me all about it after we are in the clear." Whirling, he hauled her toward the slit he had cut in the canvas but she dug in her heels.

"No, you don't! I am not going anywhere with you, you foul savage!"

"Care to bet?" Zach slugged her. He did not use all his strength, but he clipped her solidly on the jaw with enough force to cause her knees to buckle and her unconscious form to pitch against him.

Flames had engulfed the top of the bed and were licking at the tent. Already it was giving off smoke.

Zach shouldered on out, the girl a limp sack of flour. She did not stir, not even when he draped her over his saddle and swung up behind her.

From the other side of the tent came a panicked, "Oh Lord! Look there! One of the tents is on fire!"

Zach slapped his legs against the sorrel and reined to the west. He looked back when he was out of rifle range and grimly smiled. Judging by the flames shooting into the dawn sky, the fire had spread. With a little luck it would burn every tent Kilraven owned.

Zach goaded the sorrel into a gallop. He was about to race around the next hill when a rifle cracked and lead thudded into the earth in his wake. The shot came from off to his south, not from the flat-crowned hill. Dimly, he made out half a dozen riders hell-bent to cut him off. Where they had come from, he couldn't begin to guess.

Zach breathed a trifle easier when he put the next

hill between him and his pursuers. He was even more pleased when he plunged into thick forest. They would have a hard time catching him now.

The girl did not stir. Zach began to worry he had hit her too hard. He needed to check her pulse, but her wrists hung limply out of reach. It would have to wait. So would rejoining the Wards until he was sure he had given those who were after him the slip.

Zach was pleased at how well it had gone. If the Shoshones guarded their villages as poorly as Lord Kilraven did his camp, they would have been wiped out long ago.

On he rode. He saw no sign of the men who had shot at him. Evidently he had lost them.

To be safe, Zach pressed on for another quarter of an hour. A groan alerted him his captive was at last reviving. Drawing rein, he slid down and lowered her beside him. Her eyes opened, and for a few seconds she stared in confusion.

"Where am I? What is going on?"

Suddenly she remembered, because she swung an open hand at Zach's face. But her reflexes were molasses compared to his. He caught her arm and twisted, provoking a yelp.

"None of that, white woman."

"Who are you?" the girl demanded in her delightful accent.

"I am a Blackfoot," Zach said, continuing his deception. "Our war party attacked your camp."

The girl snorted. "Put a sock in it, you lying sod. You are no more a bleeding Blackfoot than I am. You're him. The one my uncle and our guide were talking about. You're Zach King."

Astonishment rendered Zach speechless.

"I'm right, aren't I, you pathetic duffer? You thought you could pull the wool over my eyes, but you can't."

"How'd you know my name?" Zach got out.

"I told you. Our guide or scout or whatever you frontier types call yourselves, he figured it out. He had Owen describe you and right away tumbled to who you are."

"Does this scout have a name?"

The girl chortled. "Of course he has a name. Everybody has a name, don't they? What do you use for brains, anyhow? Curdled milk?"

Now that he was over his initial surprise, Zach could not resist a flood of anger. "What is it?" he snapped.

Amazingly, she was not afraid. "My. Aren't we feeling formidable today? Honestly, as a terror you would make a great cowpat. You don't intimidate me, not the least little bit."

"What is *your* name? Can you spit that out without prattling like a ten-year-old?"

"Well, I never," the girl said. "For your information I happen to be Cadena Taylor, Lord Kilraven's niece. His favorite niece, I might add, in case you have dastardly designs."

"Are all British females as ridiculous as you?"

Cadena puffed out her cheeks as might an agitated chipmunk. "Oh, that is just ducky. Talk about the pot calling the kettle black. Ridiculous, am I? Says the primitive who runs around in smelly animal hides."

"The scout," Zach sought to bring her back to the

subject at hand. "You mentioned a scout working for your uncle."

"That I did, you pushy twit. Ryker. Edwin Ryker. He runs around in animals skins, too, which does not say a lot for American fashion sense."

"What in God's name are you talking about? What does fashion have to do with buckskins?"

"Nothing. Absolutely nothing at all, which is my whole point. Try to keep up. I apologize for taxing your dullard intellect, but I am making this as simple as I know how."

"Dear God." Zach had met some silly people in his time, but this girl outdid them all.

"Why do you keep bringing our Lord and Maker into this? Must you blaspheme with every other breath? I should think you would have more important matters on your mind."

"Thanks for reminding me." Abruptly spinning her around, Zach pressed her against the saddle. "Stand still."

"I bloody well will not!"

The hilt of Zach's knife molded to his palm. In a blur he pricked her neck with the tip. "I won't tell you twice. You are treating this as a lark when it is serious. Give me trouble and you will find out exactly how serious."

"You are the meanest person I have ever met," Cadena said. But she did not move or try to break free.

"In a moment you will like me even less," Zach predicted. Hunkering, he gripped the hem of her dress.

"What do you think you are doing? I will defy being ravished with my dying breath!"

"Oh, please. I would rather ravish a buffalo." Zach slashed his knife, once, twice, three times, and had the long strip he needed. Unfurling he held it for her to see. "I am going to bind your wrists. Resist, and I'll knock you over the head and bind you anyway." He tied her quickly, leaving enough excess for what he needed to do next.

"You just ruined my favorite dress."

"Keep jabbering, and I'll do worse." Zach cut off the excess and wadded the material, holding it close to his leg so she would not notice.

"You are no gentleman, sir."

"Thank God."

"There you go again. Are all heathens so irreligious?"

Zach turned her so she faced him. "Did your uncle bring you along for entertainment or did you stow away in his trunk?"

"I think I could hate you more than I have ever hated anyone," Cadena Taylor said.

"I think I could like you if I wasn't already spoken for and you did not talk like you have a pine cone up your hind end."

Cadena opened her mouth to give him a sharp retort. It was exactly what Zach expected her to do. He stuffed the wad into her mouth and jerked his fingers back before she could bite down. "Now I can have some peace and quiet."

Furious, Cadena worked her mouth, trying to spit the gag out.

"Do that," Zach said, "and instead of a piece of your dress, I will cut a piece from an old skunk hide I have in my parfleche and use that." He had no such thing. Skunks were the one animal no one bothered, for an obvious reason.

Cadena stopped moving her mouth and indulged in several hard stamps of her foot.

"You do that really well," Zach said. "It reminds me of a mare my mother had when I was little. Only the mare was better behaved."

Zach scooped her into his arm and heaved her up onto the sorrel. Or tried to. She held her legs close together and bent her knees, thwarting him. Lowering her, he tried again, with the same result.

"What the blazes do you think you are doing?" Zach demanded, and received a blank stare in return. Only then did her purpose occur to him, and he chuckled. "You can't ride sidesaddle. Not with both of us on the same horse. You must straddle the saddle like men do."

Her eyes expressed the indignation her vocal cords could not. But this time when Zach swung her up, Cadena slid one leg over the other side.

The sun had risen.

Zach rode on under a brilliant blue canopy sprinkled with puffy clouds. The green and brown of the forest and the mountains were a striking contrast. Birds warbled and chirped, welcoming the new day as was their avian custom. The air was cool but would not be so for long.

Zach reckoned it was about time he headed for the canyon where he had left the Wards. No sooner did the thought cross his mind than a rifle cracked to his rear and a lead slug buzzed within a whisker's width of his ear. Applying his heels to the sorrel, he looked back.

The six riders he had glimpsed earlier were still after him. In the lead galloped a man in buckskins. A frontiersman. Zach could not make out the man's features but he did not need to; it had to be Edwin Ryker.

Zach had only ever seen Ryker a couple of times at Bent's Fort. Ryker was one of those whites who were not fond of Indians, and even less fond of people who were half-and-half. Not that the man ever came out and said as much to Zach or anyone else. Zach saw it in the looks Ryker gave him, a look Zach knew all too well from bitter experience. The look of a bigot. Men like Ryker tried to hide it, tried to mask their feelings with oily smiles or poker faces, but Zach always knew.

Ryker had fired the shot. A man galloping next to him, a Brit, did not seem happy about it and was remonstrating with Ryker, and gesturing.

Zach pushed the sorrel to its utmost, but he was deluding himself if he thought he could outdistance them a second time. He was riding double; they were not. He had to slow them down.

A natural bench presented the opportunity. Zach came on it two-thirds of the way up the next slope. He was out of the saddle before the sorrel came to a stop. Dashing to the edge, he aimed at the lead rider's horse. He did not like to shoot horses, but Simon and Felicity wanted him to avoid spilling human blood if at all possible. The Brit spotted him, divined his intent, and sought to rein out of harm's way.

Zach stroked the trigger. At the blast, the horse squealed and stumbled. Legs flailing, it crashed down. The man threw himself clear and rolled when he hit. His horse rolled, too, toward the other riders. They sought to get of its way, but only two succeeded. The other two went down with their mounts, and Ryker was one of them.

Whirling, Zach ran to the sorrel. Cadena was slapping her legs against its sides, trying to flee, but the sorrel would not move. She kicked at Zach as he came up and almost caught him in the face. "None of that." Zach smacked her leg, none too gently. "Try it again and I will break your knee." Zach would not do any such thing, but she did not know that.

Cadena glared.

Swinging on, Zach spurred the sorrel. Once they were at the top, he stopped and reined around.

Ryker was up, but his mount was struggling to stand. So was another horse. The pair still in the saddle had stopped to render aid, but Ryker waved them on, bellowing loud enough for Zach to hear.

"After him, you yacks! Don't wait for us! Kill the bastard and save Kilraven's niece!"

Zach cupped a hand to his mouth. "Stay where you are! Don't come any higher or I'll harm the girl!" So far he had avoided taking a life, except for the horse. But if they came after him, they left him no choice. He would do what he had to do. Any blood spilled was on their shoulders, not his. His fingers flying, he began to reload the Hawken.

Cadena tried to say something through her gag, but it came out as a gurgled grunt.

The two men still on horseback were talking to the one who had remonstrated with Ryker, whose mount was on its side. Whoever the man was, he pointed up the slope.

"Damned idiots," Zach said.

The pair raised their rifles and charged him.

Chapter Twelve

"I still don't think it was right of me to let Zach go off to fight them alone," Simon Ward commented for what had to be the seventh time.

"Would it be any more right to leave me here by myself with Peter?" Felicity asked. She was tired and sore and hungry and in no mood for her husband's complaining. Seated as close to the fire as she could get without burning herself, she held her open hands to the flames to warm them.

"You're safe here," Simon replied. "Zach said so."

"We're safe so long as no beasts or hostiles happen by," Felicity amended. She yearned for an hour's sleep. Just one hour. But she could not bring herself to lie down. She was worried about Zach, worried about their cabin, worried about her son, and, yes, worried about her husband.

"Nothing has so far," Simon said. And the sun would be up any minute.

At that exact instant, from somewhere up the

canyon, wafted a low growl. It brought Simon to his feet with his hand on the hilt of the butcher knife wedged under his belt. He had grabbed the knife when they were packing to leave. "I wish Kilraven hadn't taken all our guns."

"That makes two of us." Felicity gazed up the canyon, but whatever growled was not close enough to see. Balling her fists, she glanced at Peter to confirm he was still blissfully asleep.

"Wild animals don't like fire," Simon remarked to set her at ease. "Whatever is out there will leave us be." *But what if it doesn't?* he asked himself. Suddenly the butcher knife seemed puny.

Felicity stared into the flames. She would give anything to be snug and warm and safe back in their cabin. She said so aloud.

"I know how you feel," Simon responded.

One of the horses whinnied.

Both Simon and Felicity turned and saw that the entire string had their heads up and their ears pricked and were staring intently into the dark. The picket rope jiggled as one of the horses shied a few steps back.

"Watch they don't run off," Felicity urged. The only thing worse than being in the wild without guns was being stranded afoot in the wild without guns.

"They're not going anywhere." Simon had picketed them himself. The picket rope was secure.

A second horse nickered. Almost immediately another growl came out of the night, much closer than before, so close that there could be no doubt the thing was watching them and perhaps making up its mind whether to attack.

"What do you think it is?" Felicity whispered, sliding near to Peter and tenderly placing her hand on his sleeping form.

"How should I know?" Simon was not sufficiently versed in the sounds animals made to tell a grizzly's growl from a black bear's or a mountain lion's from a bobcat's.

"Make the fire bigger," Felicity suggested. "Add more wood."

Simon quickly complied. He did not point out that Zach had advised them to keep the fire small so roving war parties would not spot it. The flames leaped, sending fiery embers into the air and casting their radiance an additional thirty feet.

Felicity gasped.

At very edge of the light glowed a pair of feral eyes. Slanted eyes that burned red like the eyes of some demon. "There!" she cried, pointing.

Simon had seen them. He remembered that bear eyes were round, so these did not belong to a bear. He also remembered that cat eyes slanted, which suggested, given their size, that they were the eyes of a mountain lion. Some of his fear dissolved. The big cats were not prone to attack human beings.

The eyes blinked.

A shiver ran down Felicity's spine. Why, she couldn't say, unless it was the horror of being sized up for a meal by the unknown.

Simon decided to try a bluff. Bending down, he gripped a burning brand by the unlit end, held it aloft, and advanced several steps toward the nocturnal prowler. His hope was to scare it off.

Just like that, the eyes were gone.

"You chased it away!" Felicity squealed in delight, and clapped her hands as if she were applauding a scene in a play. Peter stirred and mumbled. Not wanting to wake him, she stopped clapping. "I guess it's true. Wild animals really are afraid of fire."

Pleased by his little triumph, Simon placed the brand back in the fire. "I will do it again if it comes back." He did not really expect the thing to return. Which made his shock all the more severe when he gazed past his wife and beheld the red eyes peering at them from the other side of their camp. The thing had not left; it had circled around.

Felicity noticed his expression. "What is it?" she asked. Turning, she let out a gasp. The eyes were no more than fifteen feet out. Once again they blinked. Once again a shiver rippled the length of her spine. "Oh God."

"Let's not panic," Simon said. There was only one of whatever it was. Surely he could handle one. He scooped up a brand and brought it around, holding it high as he had done before. "Go away! Shoo!"

"You'll wake up Peter," Felicity said.

The eyes blinked.

"It's not leaving." Simon palmed the butcher knife. "Stay here. I'll try to drive it off."

Pushing to her feet, Felicity caught hold of his arm. "You're not going anywhere. We don't know what it is or what it will do."

"I scared it off once," Simon said. He looked at her hand until she reluctantly removed it. Extending the knife, and with the burning brand held high, Simon warily edged toward those gleaming eyes.

The animal did not move.

"Simon, I don't like this," Felicity said anxiously. "What if you make it mad and it attacks?"

That gave Simon pause. Nate King once told him that most animals ran at the sight of humans. Of those that didn't, most would run off if yelled at. Of *those* that didn't, nine times out of ten they could be bluffed into fleeing. "The important thing," Nate had related, "is never show fear. Never, ever let on that you are afraid. Animals can sense it. They can smell it. And when a meat eater smells fear, it's the same as ringing the dinner bell."

Simon swallowed hard. He was trying to put on a bold front but he *was* more than a little afraid, more for them than for himself. The thing might sense it. He had to do something. So he continued to slowly advance, all the while praying the creature would run off.

Another growl filled the air, a low, ominous rumble that hinted the beast was not going anywhere. Stopping, he waved the brand and winced when a red hot sliver fell on his hand. "Get out of here!" he yelled. "Go eat a deer or something!"

Instead of fleeing, the thing lowered its head and took a few steps toward him.

Simon halted. His bluff had not worked. The flickering torchlight suggested the creature was crouched low to the ground, poised to pounce. He still could not tell what animal they were dealing with.

"Simon?" Felicity said uncertainly. She had moved

between the thing and their son so that to get at Peter it had to go through her. "Back away. Come over here with us."

Good advice, Simon thought. But to his horror, each time he took a step back, the thing took a step forward. He stopped after three steps, unwilling to draw it closer. But the thing did not stop. It kept slinking toward him.

The eastern sky had been brightening the whole while. Between the harbinger of dawn and Simon's brand, he finally saw the creature clearly enough to identify it. "No!" he breathed.

It was a wolf.

A huge timber wolf.

Zach King had been taught to load a rifle when he was barely big enough to hold one. The routine was always the same; open the powder horn, pour the powder down the barrel, open the ammo pouch, take out a ball and patch, use the ramrod to tamp the ball and patch down the barrel, cock and fire. He had done it so many times he could do it half-asleep in the dark. He could do it quickly, too, so quickly that the two men charging him were only halfway to the bench when he fired. His slug caught the man on the right high in the shoulder, the impact knocking him from the saddle. The second rider snapped off a shot of his own, but he was shooting on the fly from a moving mount and his aim was atrocious.

Zach did not have time to reload the Hawken. He drew a pistol, aimed, and fired when the rider was less than fifteen feet below. The man screeched as he catapulted to the ground.

Cadena gurgled something, her eyes hurling twin daggers at him.

The men lower down started firing.

Zach got out of there. He rode for half an hour, until he was sure they were not being chased. Only then did he deem it safe to slow to a walk. "Do you want the gag out?"

The girl gurgled anew.

"I'll take it out," Zach offered. "But if you try to bite me or act up in any way, I'll put it back in and leave it in until you starve to death. Savvy?"

Her eyes flashing, Cadena nodded. As soon as the gag was removed, she coughed and worked her jaw up and down. "You are a brute. A vile, awful brute."

"My wife doesn't think so." Zach clucked to the sorrel.

"Is she feeble witted?" Cadena scoffed.

"Louisa is as fine a woman as ever lived," Zach said proudly. "She is as smart as you and as pretty, besides."

"So you say, but I cannot help but question the judgment of any woman who would pick you when there are so many better men in the world."

Zach did not take offense. He admired the girl's spunk. "If your tongue were any sharper, you'd cut your mouth when you talk."

For a space they rode quietly, the warmth of the morning growing, the forest around them alive with the sounds of birds and squirrels and the occasional squawk of a jay or the caw of a raven.

Zach kept an eye on their back trail, but his enemies had apparently learned from the clash and given up.

"Why do you do this?" Cadena unexpectedly asked.

"Why have I taken you?"

"No. Why do you oppose my uncle. You cannot possibly prevail. You are one against many."

"I told you. The Wards are friends of my family, and we stand by our friends. If my pa was here instead of me, he would do the same."

"You value friendships that much, do you?" Cadena inquired, no trace of sarcasm in her tone.

"Don't you?" Zach rejoined. "But yes, I do. I don't have so many friends that I can afford to lose any." He grinned. "You might find this hard to believe, but I don't make friends easy."

"Now that I can understand," Cadena said, and she grinned, too.

"A lot has to do with what I am," Zach mentioned. "Breeds are not held in high regard in these parts."

"Breeds?" Cadena repeated.

"Half-breeds, some call us. A mix of white blood and red blood. Or it could be white and Mexican. Hell, any mix, and most whites think you're vermin." Zach felt himself becoming angry and stopped.

"Ah. Class distinctions. We have them in England, too. I happen to be in the privileged class, and I can't say I would have it any other way. I like having the best clothes and the best food and the best of everything else."

"At least you're honest about it."

"Why shouldn't I be? There is no shame in being born into wealth and influence. We are what we are, as my uncle is fond of saying. He wields a lot of power and has no qualms about doing so."

"It doesn't give him the right to force people from their home," Zach said. "It doesn't give him the right to steal their land out from under them."

"In the first place, my uncle offered them a fair price for their homestead. I was there. I heard him. But they refused to sell."

"They don't have to if they don't want to."

"In the second place, as I understand it, they do not have a strict legal claim to the valley. No government record exists of their ownership. It is theirs only because they say it is."

"That is more than enough." Zach looked at her. "It is not the same here as it is in your country or back East. Out here we don't have any government. There is no place to file on land. A man takes what he wants, so long as it does not belong to someone else." That would change eventually. His father had heard that Congress was considering some sort of homestead act that would bring rules and regulations to the frontier.

"That is not entirely true, is it?" Cadena countered. "The Indians were here first. So any land white men claim is land that belongs to the Indians. Where is the distinction between what you and the Wards have done and what my uncle is doing?"

"Most Indians do not think of land the same way whites do. Each tribe has a territory, but the territory belongs to the whole tribe. With whites, each person wants his own little patch."

"Which do you prefer? The white way or the Indian way?"

Zach had never given it much thought. He had a cabin, but the valley in which he lived was shared by his parents and their best friend and his wife and another family. "I live both ways."

They came to a clearing. Cadena squirmed in the saddle, then asked, "I don't suppose you would be kind enough to loosen my wrists? You tied them so tight, you cut off the circulation. My arms hurt."

"I reckon I could," Zach allowed. "So long as you continue to behave." Drawing rein, he dismounted and reached up to lower her to the ground. "You can stretch your legs if you want." It would be an hour or so until they reached the canyon.

Just then, behind him, a gun hammer clicked. "Give me an excuse, and I'll blow you to hell."

Chapter Thirteen

Simon Ward's initial shock gave way to relief. According to Nate King, wolves rarely attacked humans. Nate knew of only two instances. The first involved the Crows and took place long ago during a particularly severe winter. A pack of starving wolves had attacked a hunting party and been driven off. The second time was when a trapper came on a mother wolf with young ones and the mother wolf leaped at him, plainly to defend her offspring.

"Get back here!" Felicity urged. The wolf terrified her. It was far bigger than any dog, and when it snarled, it bared a mouthful of razor fangs. Scooping Peter into her arms, she stood.

Simon slowly backed toward her, saying, "I don't think we have anything to worry about. It's only a wolf."

"Why doesn't it run off? Is it rabid?"

Simon gave a start. He had not considered that.

But rabid animals foamed at the mouth and behaved bizarrely, and the wolf was neither foaming nor acting strangely. On an impulse he threw the brand at it, thinking the fire would drive it off. The wolf skipped nimbly aside and resumed its slow, slinking advance.

"We must do something," Felicity urged.

"I'm open to suggestions," Simon said. By now the sky had brightened enough that he could see the wolf clearly. He was struck by how gaunt it was, virtually skin and bones, and by the gray streaks along its muzzle and face. Now he understood. The wolf was old and desperately hungry and saw them as easy prey.

Felicity cast about for a weapon. The best she could do was a piece of wood Simon had gathered for the fire. A foot long and as thick as her wrist, it made a stout club.

Simon sidled to the fire. Without taking his eyes off the wolf, he stooped and picked up another burning brand, nearly burning his fingers in the process. He waved it at the wolf, but the wolf paid no heed. "If it attacks, run."

"And leave you to fight it alone?" Felicity shook her head. "I am your wife. I will stay by your side."

"Please," Simon said. "We have Peter to think off. Climb a tree. You will be safe in a tree."

"No."

"I am not asking you, I am telling you. For my sake as well as yours. I can't fight this thing and protect you, both." Simon brandished his knife at the wolf, but it might as well have been a toothpick for all the effect it had.

"You need someone to watch your back," Felicity admonished.

"Damn it." Simon had more to say, a lot more, but the wolf chose that moment to crouch lower and growl. Its belly was virtually touching the ground and its tail had gone rigid.

"It's getting ready to attack," Felicity warned.

Simon thought so, too. He moved in front of her, ignoring her question of "What do you think you're doing?" He focused on the wolf and only the wolf.

Felicity went to step out from behind him, but didn't. She could not do much with Peter in her arms. Better to hold herself in reserve, she decided, until her husband needed her.

The wolf sidled to the left.

Simon moved in the direction the wolf was moving, keeping his wife and son behind him. When the wolf stopped, he stopped. When it resumed circling, he circled with it. The tension ate at him like acid.

"What if we both rush it at once?" Felicity proposed.

"No."

"That might be all it takes." Felicity refused to believe the wolf would stand up to both of them.

"Rush it with Peter in your arms?" Simon thrust the brand at their lupine nemesis, but the wolf held its ground. "Come up with something better."

"But there *is* nothing better," Felicity said. Not that she could think of, anyway.

That was when Simon noticed the wolf was craning its neck as if trying to see past him. Meat eaters always went after the easiest prey, or so everyone claimed. He jumped to the conclusion it was after

Felicity, and not him. Then Peter mumbled in his sleep, and the wolf pricked its ears and snarled. "God in heaven," he blurted in alarm.

"What?"

An icy fist had closed around Simon's heart. "It's after Peter." Exactly as the wolf would go after a fawn if it encountered a bunch of deer, or after a calf if it came across buffalo.

Felicity clasped her son tighter to her and leaned to one side to better see the wolf. "What makes you say that?"

"Take a step to the right and I will take one to the left and watch what the wolf does."

"Short steps," Felicity cautioned. She did as he had instructed, and sure enough, the wolf's gaze was glued to her and not to Simon. Specifically, its gaze was glued to the child in her arms. "No!" she breathed, overcome by terror. She nearly spun and bolted. Peter was her bundle of joy, part of her heart-given flesh and form. She loved him just as any mother loved her child, completely and unreservedly. She could not countenance the thought of him coming to harm. His pain was her pain. His death unthinkable. Rage boiled in her, rage that this wolf would dare want to devour him, rage so potent that she whirled and shoved Peter into Simon's startled grasp. "Don't let anything happen to him."

"Why are you giving him to—?" Simon began, and was rendered momentarily speechless.

Felicity, gripping her club in both hands, flew at the wolf. She shrieked as she sprang forward, a wail of fury torn from her soul. The wolf growled and coiled to spring, and then she was on it, swinging her club, seeking to bash in its head and dash out its brains.

But she was not quick enough.

With deceptive ease the wolf danced aside. It nipped at her leg but missed. Her club caught it on the shoulder, a glancing blow, and the wolf yipped and retreated, but only a few feet. Halting, it stared at her, almost as if it were taunting her to try again.

Felicity did. Emboldened that she had forced it to give way, she ran toward it with her club raised to strike. Suddenly the wolf exploded into motion, coming straight at her. She tensed to bring the club smashing down, but the wolf veered and swept past her in a blur of teeth and hair. Too late, she divined its true intent.

The wolf was not after her.

It was streaking toward her husband—and Peter.

Zach King froze. He did not doubt the speaker would do exactly as he threatened to do. "Let me guess," he said calmly, although his insides were churning. "Edwin Ryker."

"Who else? Drop your Hawken, hold your arms out from your sides, and slowly turn around."

Cadena grinned in spiteful glee. "Let me hear more of your bluster and bravado now."

Zach did as Ryker had directed. He felt like a dunce, being taken this way. "I thought I lost you."

Striding out of the trees with his rifle leveled, Ryker rasped, "I had to shoot my horse because of you, you son of a bitch. When it fell, it broke a leg." He had helped himself to a mount belonging to one of the Brit's and come on alone. Instead of trailing them and possibly being spotted, he had taken a gamble. He nearly rode the horse to exhaustion in a wide loop that brought him to a point ahead of King and the girl.

"I didn't kill you," Zach said. In hindsight, he should have.

"Drop the pistols and the knife," Ryker directed. "Real slow, if you know what's good for you." He sighted down his rifle. "You'll live a little longer if you do."

Simmering inside, Zach obeyed.

Ryker smirked. "Which knee should I shoot out first? Your right or your left?"

Zach steeled himself to leap the instant the rifle went off. They were close enough that he might reach Ryker even if he was hit.

"Or should I get it over with right away?" Ryker taunted. "Put a slug between your eyes, say? Or through the heart?"

"No," Cadena Taylor said.

Without looking at her, Ryker asked, "What in hell do you mean by no? Your uncle sent me to track down this breed and the Wards, and to do as I damn well please with them."

"I will thank you to stop swearing," Cadena said sternly. "Perhaps in your country it is acceptable to be uncouth in the presence of a lady, but in my country it is not."

"You are not *in* your country," Ryker snapped. He never had cottoned to her. In his estimation she was a snot-nosed uppity bitch.

"But *you* are in my uncle's employ, and as his niece, I have a say in what you do."

Ryker had half a mind to haul her from the saddle and slap her until she begged for mercy. "I answer to your uncle, not to you," he said. "Give me one good reason why I should keep this breed alive."

"Are the Wards reason enough?"

"How do they fit in?"

"Do you know where they are?" Cadena asked.

"Not yet. I'll find them, though. It might take a few days, depending on how well hid they are. But they're as good as caught."

"Why go to all that bother when there is an easier way?" Cadena argued. She nodded at Zach. "He knows where they are. We will take him back to my uncle and let my uncle get the information out of him. My uncle will like that very much." She stressed that last part. "You see, I happen to know something about him that you do not."

"What would that be?"

"My uncle has a sadistic streak. He likes nothing better than to whip a man to the bone. I have seen him do it, seen how immensely he enjoyed the whipping." Cadena smiled sweetly. "It would be a shame to deprive him of so much fun by killing Zach King outright."

Ryker regarded her thoughtfully. "You call whipping a man fun? Do you like hurting things, too, lady?"

"I like it very much," Cadena said coolly, and looked at Zach. "After the indignities he has heaped on me, I can't wait to have him writhe in the utmost pain he has ever experienced."

"I'll be," Ryker said, and laughed. "You're a female after my own heart. Too bad you're not older."

"If I were, you would be the last person on earth I would be intimate with, if that is what you are implying." Cadena pumped her arms. "Now would you be so kind as to untie me?"

Zach was made to lie on his stomach with his arms spread wide. He did not resist. Ryker would shoot him without a moment's hesitation. Zach preferred to stay in one piece until the right time and place presented itself. His cheek on the ground, he watched as Ryker helped Cadena down and slit the strip that bound her wrists with a deft slash of his blade.

Rubbing her wrists, Cadena walked over to Zach. "Now it is my turn, you bloody savage."

Zach glanced up just as her foot connected with his ribs. His whole side exploded with agony. Involuntarily, he started to double over but turned to stone at a cold command from Ryker.

"Stay exactly as you are or I'll shoot you in the leg. She wants you alive to torture, but she hasn't said you have to be intact."

Cadena smiled. "You have a mean streak too, I notice, Mr. Ryker."

"I do what needs doing."

Zach endured two more kicks, each harder than the last. It was all he could do to breathe, and pinpoints of light swirled before his eyes. If one of his ribs wasn't cracked, it was a miracle. He glared at Cadena. He had treated her decent enough, all things considered, and this was how she repaid him.

"Don't look at me like that," Cadena snapped. "What else did you expect? You struck me, remember, back in the tent? You dragged me off against my will. You bound me like some common criminal. Did you think I would not resent it? Did you think I would forgive and forget?" Cadena's laugh was ice and hate in equal measure. "You miserable provincial. I suppose you cannot help being as stupid as you are, given the heathen inheritance that flows through your veins. But honestly, you are pathetic."

Zach did not give her the satisfaction of responding.

"Cat have your tongue?" Cadena bated him. "Very well. Pretend it doesn't matter. Pretend my barbs don't sting. I know better." She drew back her leg to kick him again but abruptly changed her mind. "No. We will save the pain for when you reach our camp. It will give you something to look forward to."

Both Cadena and Ryker laughed.

Zach did not resist as his wrists were tied behind his back. Cadena covered him with one of his own pistols while Ryker did the tying. It was Ryker who stripped him of his possibles bag, ammo pouch and powder horn, Ryker who slung him, belly down, over his saddle.

The ride to the flat-topped hill seemed to take forever, but it was not yet noon when they arrived.

All the tents had burned to the ground. The fire had spread from one to the other so rapidly, few of Lord Kilraven's personal possessions were saved.

A sentry gave a shout, and Kilraven and his wife were waiting to meet them. Zach had never felt so helpless. He tried to slide down of his own accord but Ryker gripped him by the back of his shirt and dumped him in the dirt.

"What have we here?" Lord Kilraven asked.

"A present for you, Uncle," Cadena said. "For you

to do with as you please. Do you still have that whip you are so fond of?"

"As a matter of fact," Lord Kilraven replied. "It was in one of the packs outside when the tent burned." He grinned down at Zach. "I can hardly wait to use it."

Chapter Fourteen

Simon Ward had a split second in which to act. The wolf was almost on them when, with the fervent hope Peter would not be hurt, Simon swiveled at the hips and dropped his son behind him.

It was too late for the wolf to stop. It had already launched itself into the air.

Simon met the leap head-on. The wolf was skin and bones, but its sinews still retained much of their raw power, and it still weighed well over a hundred pounds. Simon was sent stumbling by the impact and tripped over Peter. Even as he fell, he gripped the wolf's throat and twisted to one side to fall clear of his son. He nearly had his wrist ripped open by a snap of the wolf's iron jaws. Searing heat and pain shot up his legs, and too late he realized he had fallen into the fire. He rolled, hauling the wolf with him, the wolf snarling and thrashing and striving its utmost to bite him.

Then they were out of the fire and still rolling. Simon thrust the butcher knife into the wolf, and it snapped at his face, at his throat. Suddenly a cold liquid sensation enveloped him. They had rolled into the spring. In a twinkling the wolf's fur was as slick as axle grease. Simon lost his hold.

Simon had no idea how deep the spring was. He thrust his legs down to find purchase, but his feet did not touch bottom.

The wolf was a crazed demon, struggling fiercely to break free while snapping and clawing in a frenzy.

Pain flared in Simon's chest and thighs. The wolf's claws were shredding his clothes and gouging his flesh. He stabbed and stabbed and stabbed, the spring roiling around them, barely able to keep his head above water. He stabbed the wolf over a dozen times. Again and again the wolf's fangs gnashed within inches of his jugular.

Simon tried not to swallow water but could not help doing so. The water, red water, got into his nose, choking off his breath. It got into his eyes, blurring his vision. Everything blurred: the wolf, the spring, the world. But still Simon stabbed and stabbed and stabbed, until his arms were leaden, until he was so spent he did not have enough strength to raise the knife. His body sagged and his head drooped, and he felt himself slowly sinking.

A sharp tug on his shirt restored Simon to some semblance of awareness. He was pulled upward and over to the edge so that he lay with half his body out of the water and half his body in. Sputtering and coughing, he blinked and gazed about him.

Felicity was at his side. "I thought I had lost you,"

she said tremulously. "I thought all that blood was yours."

Simon looked at the spring. The water was scarlet. The wolf floated a few feet away, head down, its gaunt form riddled with puncture wounds. Suddenly Simon stiffened. "Peter?" he gasped.

"You saved him," Felicity said. She reached out an arm and pulled the boy to her. He was rubbing his eyes and yawning and did not seem to realize what had happened.

Simon crawled out of the spring and sat up, his arms behind him to brace him so he did not slump in exhaustion. "Are you all right, son?"

"Yes, Pa," the boy answered. "Why are you wet?"

"I was wrestling a wolf."

Peter stared at the still form in the water. "You wrestle real good."

"Is there anything I can get you?" Felicity asked. "Bandages? Dry clothes? Coffee? Anything at all?"

"After a bit," Simon said. His arms had begun to shake. He lay back, totally spent, and stared at the sky. What a way to start the new day, he thought, and grinned. He closed his eyes. He would lie there a few minutes and then get up and change.

"Simon?"

"Yes, dear," Simon heard himself mumble.

"It is almost noon. You really should get out of those damp clothes and have some of the soup I've made."

Simon opened his eyes and was stunned to see the sun almost directly overhead. "I passed out!"

Felicity smiled and tenderly placed a hand on his forehead. "You were sleeping so peacefully, I didn't have the heart to disturb you." Most of the time she had sat watching him sleep, grateful he was alive.

The aroma of the coffee brought Simon up on his elbows. His stomach rumbled, reminding him of how hungry he was. Peter was over by the fire, drawing in the dirt with a stick. "Zach?"

"There has been no sign of him. I am worried." Felicity almost said "very worried."

Simon moved his right hand and bumped a neatly folded pile of clothes she had set next to him. It was only then that he discovered he was still clutching the butcher knife in his right hand. He let it drop and flexed his stiff fingers.

"We have another problem," Felicity said, and indicated the spring.

Simon regarded the red water and the body floating in the middle, and nodded his understanding.

"We have one half-full water skin and that is it," Felicity said. "The horses will be thirsty before too long. What do we do?"

The nearest water that Simon knew of was the stream that nurtured their valley. "I'll have some of that coffee now."

"I added sugar the way you like it."

Simon sipped, savoring the warmth that spread down his throat and into his stomach. He took his time, mulling their options, and after draining the last drop, voiced his opinion. "We cannot stay here."

"I agree."

"We have to go back. It was wrong of us to let Zach do our fighting for us. We should never have let him go off alone."

"Again, I agree."

"We'll find a spot where Peter and you can hide, and I will sneak as close as I can get to Kilraven's camp."

"This time I don't agree," Felicity said.

"Why not?"

"We are a family. We should stick together. We'll hide the horses, and I will go with you."

"And Peter?"

"He goes with us. I'll watch over him." Felicity took the tin cup and stepped to the coffeepot to refill it. As she brought it back she said, "No argument?"

"I have been pondering," Simon said. "The reason we have been driven from our home, the reason we're hiding here like hunted animals, is due to Lord Kilraven."

"I'm not sure I follow you." To Felicity, he was merely stating the obvious.

"Kilraven is the key. The hunting preserve is his idea. Driving us from our valley is his idea. His wife and his niece and all those others are here because of him."

"So?"

"So if he dies, the rest will pack up and go back to England."

Felicity let the full implication sink in. "You intend to kill him?"

"I do," Simon said. It was the solution, the *only* solution, to their ordeal. "With him gone things will go back to being as they were."

"Killing a wolf is one thing," Felicity commented. "Killing a human being is another."

"It has to be done," Simon insisted. "God knows, I

did not ask for this. Kilraven has brought it down on his own head."

"How will you kill him without a rifle or a pistol?" Felicity asked. "I doubt he would let you get close enough to use the knife."

"I'll think of something," Simon assured her. He clasped her hand. "Are we agreed in this, too? For the sake of our family, for the sake of our future, Lord Kilraven must die?"

"We are agreed," Felicity Ward said.

The sun burned hot on Zach King's back. His ribs throbbed with pain. His wrists were rubbed raw, and blood dripped from the ropes that dug into his flesh. He licked his dry lips and squinted up at the blazing orb. "A pox on all suns."

Zach was naked from the waist up, his wrists lashed to thick posts imbedded firmly in the earth. Beads of sweat dotted his brow and were trickling down his face. One of those drops trickled into his right eye, stinging terribly.

Zach glared at the nearest fire and the people ringing it. They were talking and joking and laughing. Whenever one of them was thirsty, they held out their glass and a servant was ready with a pitcher.

Zach sensed rather than heard someone come up next to him. Her perfume told him who it was. "You again."

"Enjoying yourself?" Saxona Kilraven asked. She wore a long dress with frills and tiny buttons. Her hair was perfectly in place. Her teeth, when her lips curled in a mocking smile, were dazzling white.

"Go to hell."

"Is that any way to talk to a lady?" Saxona asked, sounding genuinely offended.

"My wife is a lady. My mother is a lady. You are a conniving bitch with a whoreson for a husband. You are both going to die."

Saxona laughed. "Bold words for one so helpless. Before this day is out, it is very likely you are the one who will be dead."

Zach looked at her. "Why do you keep coming over here? Does it amuse you?"

"Very much," Saxona admitted. "We do not have your kind in my country. I find you fascinating. You possess an animal quality that is quite unique."

"I am no different from anyone else," Zach said harshly. Being branded a breed was bad enough; being called an animal rankled.

"On the contrary," Saxona said. "But then, you have not seen as much of the world as I have. The true Indians of India, the natives of Africa, the countries of the Mediterranean, such a marvelous diversity of people."

Zach did not see what she was getting at and did not care. "How long is your husband going to keep me tied to these posts?"

"Why don't you ask him? Here he comes now."

Lord Kilraven was strolling toward them, a full glass of water in his hand. "How are the two of you getting along?" he asked congenially. "Are you the best of friends by now?"

"Oh, husband," Saxona said, and laughed.

Kilraven made a show of slowly raising the glass to his mouth and taking a sip. He sighed in contentment and remarked, "There is nothing like water on a hot day like today." He extended the glass toward Zach. "Would you care for some?"

Saxona tittered merrily.

Zach contained his fury with an effort. He looked away from them, only to see Edwin Ryker and Cadena approaching. The girl had spent a lot of time in Ryker's company since their return.

"Still just hanging there, I see," the frontiersman said to Zach, and turned to Kilraven. "When does the whipping commence? The sooner you make him talk, the sooner I bring the Wards to heel."

"You must learn to be more patient," Lord Kilraven said. "The anticipation of pain is almost as exquisite a torment as the actual inflicting of pain itself. I have given our young friend these past few hours to think about what is in store for him. Trust me when I say it will make the whipping that much worse."

"Not with the breed it won't," Ryker said. "He's as tough as rawhide, this one. You may not get a peep out of him."

"Nonsense. You will see for yourself shortly." Kilraven switched his attention to his niece. "And how are you, my dear? We have not seen much of you since you were rescued."

"I went on a walk with Edwin," Cadena said. "He is teaching me about America."

"Is he, indeed?" Saxona said.

Lord Kilraven's features hardened. "Be advised, young lady, that when in Rome, we do not do as the Romans do."

Cadena blushed. Ryker glanced from her to her uncle and said, "Care to explain that for those of us who don't know Romans from Russians?"

"I refer to the fact that although we are not in Britain, we do not forsake British customs. Class distinctions hold as true here as they do over there. More so, if one is to preserve her dignity." Kilraven gave his niece a pointed stare, and she averted her eyes.

"I'm not so sure I like what you're saying," Ryker said.

"My dear fellow," Kilraven said suavely, "your likes and dislikes are of no relevance whatsoever. You were hired to do a job and that is the extent of your influence. The rest of the time you mean no more to me than, say, our pack horses."

Now it was Ryker who turned the same hue as a beet. "I don't like being insulted, mister. I don't care who you are."

"What does it take to make myself clear?" Kilraven responded. "You are a hireling. Nothing more. Your cares are of absolutely no consequence."

Ryker balled his fists. "If you weren't paying me so much extra, I'd teach you a thing or two."

"I am not paying you a cent more than we initially agreed," Lord Kilraven informed him.

"What? You promised me five thousand dollars if I went after King and the Wards."

"Correction," Kilraven said. "I promised you five thousand if you eliminated them. But the Wards are still out there somewhere, and Zach King is still breathing."

"I brought him back for you!" Ryker fumed, and jabbed a thumb at Cadena. "It was her idea. She said you would want me to so you could have some fun with him."

"Ah, well," Kilraven said. "Even so, I can hardly

justify paying you the extra money when you have clearly not earned it."

"You don't want to do this," Ryker warned.

"Sure I do." Lord Kilraven motioned at where Severn and Bromley and several others were watching and listening, all armed with rifles. "And I have the means to enforce my decision."

Without another word, Edwin Ryker spun and stormed off.

"Now then," Lord Kilraven said, facing Zach. "Shall we get to it?" He raised his voice. "Mr. Severn, bring my whip, if you please. And Mr. Meldon, fetch a tumbler of salt."

Chapter Fifteen

Zach King thought he knew pain. Over the years he had suffered a number of wounds and injuries. He had been bitten, clawed, nearly torn to pieces by a wolverine. He had been cut. He had been clubbed. Pain, in all its guises. But he was mistaken. He did not really know pain. He did not know pain at all.

The first bite of the leather whip seared his body with molten fire. He had steeled himself, but he still arched his back and had to grit his teeth to keep from crying out.

Mirth greeted his torment. Everyone except the sentries had gathered to witness the whipping. The maids pointed and giggled. Cadena Taylor grinned. Saxona Kilraven smiled. Many of the men laughed. Only one person did not share their delight, only one person was scowling, and that, ironically enough, was Edwin Ryker.

Zach sucked air into his lungs and calmed himself. He had endured one blow, he could endure fifty.

But thinking he could and doing it proved to be a case of wishful thinking.

The second stroke seared Zach much like the first. The third hurt more. The sixth was agony. The tenth, excruciating. By the twentieth he was barely conscious. He did not realize the whipping had stopped until a hand cupped his chin and lifted his head.

"Are you still alive?" Lord Kilraven grinned. "Good. It would not do to kill you too soon. For the inconvenience you have caused me, you must take a long time dying. A very long time, indeed." He stepped back. "Mr. Bromley, if you please."

To Zach's amazement, a glass was pressed to his lips. He gulped reflexively, and coughed.

"Not too much, Mr. Bromley," Kilraven commanded. "Just enough to restore him." He snapped his fingers. "Mr. Severn, it is your turn. Be liberal with your sprinkling."

Zach yearned for more water. He paid no attention as Severn walked behind him. But he did when a strange sensation spread across his back. The only thing he could compare it to was the time his family traveled to Oregon Country, and the Pacific coast. One day on the beach his sister had poured sand on his back while he lay sunning himself and watching seals frolic. The sensation was the same.

Then the pain hit him. Zach remembered Kilraven mentioning something about a tumbler of salt. *Severn was sprinkling salt on his wounds!* He tried to draw away but the ropes held him fast. Racked by the most acute anguish he had ever experienced, he writhed and twisted from side to side, the whole while he bit his lower lip so as not to scream.

Many of the onlookers laughed. Lord Kilraven was happily smiling. Saxona's eyes glittered, and her bosom rose and fell.

Pain, pain, and more pain. Pain that would not stop. Pain so potent, it filled every fiber of Zach's being. He no longer saw the people watching or the sky or the ground. He saw a white haze of pain. He wanted to shriek his head off. God, how he wanted to! He clamped his teeth on his lip until blood flowed and then gnashed his teeth until they were fit to break in half, and not once did he let out a sound.

Eventually, sweet unconsciousness claimed him. Zach's body sagged. Mentally, he drifted in a limbo of agony.

Again, it was a hand on his chin that brought Zach back to the world of the living. He thought it must be Kilraven. As sluggish as molasses, he raised his head. The sun was well on its westward arc. Most of the afternoon was gone. "Come to gloat?" he croaked after five tries.

"No," Edwin Ryker said, glancing about them. "Keep your voice down. If his highness sees me talking to you without his say-so, he is liable to throw a fit."

Zach swallowed a few times to moisten his parched throat. "What do you want?"

Ryker leaned closer. "If you were free would you kill me?"

"So fast your head would swim," Zach vowed.

"But what if it was *me* who set you free?" Ryker asked. "Would you still want me dead?"

Zach forced his mind to function. The frontiersman was serious. "What are you up to? You are the one who brought me here."

Suddenly Ryker stepped back. Several servants walked past and he smiled and said, "How do you do?" They did not acknowledge his greeting but treated him as if he were not there. When they were out of earshot, he came close to Zach again. "Does that answer your question?"

"Not really."

"I'm tired of how they treat me. I'm tired of Mr. High-and-Mighty acting as if I'm not fit to lick his boots. As much as I'd like to carve on him with my knife, it would buy me too much trouble. So I'll do the next best thing. I'll cut you loose."

"That's only part of it," Zach guessed. "You want to get back at Kilraven for not paying you the five thousand dollars."

"What difference does it make *why* I help you so long as I do? But I need your word that you won't come after me. I want your solemn oath you will not kill me."

Zach glanced at the ropes binding his wrists. All he had to do was agree and he would be free. It entailed swallowing his pride, though. It entailed doing something he had never done before: letting someone who had done him wrong live. He turned to answer and discovered that Ryker had backed away a couple of steps and was gazing off to the east. "What are you doing?" he asked.

A shadow fell between them.

"That is what I would like to know," Lord Kilraven said. "Why are you over here, Mr. Ryker? I gave specific instructions no one was to come anywhere near my guest without my express permission."

"Guest?" Zach spat. "Captive is more like it."

"If it helps," Kilraven said sarcastically, "think of yourself as a sacrifice on the road to progress. A year from now, when my hunting lodge has been built and hunters flock from all over the world to test the fabled bounty of these mountains, I will drink a toast to your health."

"You will be bleached bones by then," Zach said.

Kilraven turned to Ryker. "I still await your reply. What are you doing here?" Behind him appeared Severn, Owen, and others.

Ryker hooked his thumbs in his belt. "I was rubbing the breed's nose in the fact his time on this earth is about up. What is wrong with that?"

"You have not been listening," Kilraven responded. "You did not ask my consent. See that in the future you do exactly as I say or you will not like the consequences."

Shrugging, Ryker walked off.

Lord Kilraven gestured toward Severn. "My whip, if you please. Our captive, as he prefers to call himself, has revived sufficiently. It is time for his next whipping."

Simon and Felicity left the pack animals in pines half a mile from the flattopped hill. It went against every dictate of logic Simon possessed for him to leave the horses untended. Most Indian tribes considered stealing a horse high on their list of feats worthy of counting coup. But it would be impossible

for Felicity and him to get anywhere near the hill
unless they went in quick and quiet, and that meant
taking their mounts and leaving the rest.

"I don't suppose you would consider staying with
the horses?" Simon had asked.

"You know better," Felicity said.

Simon had sighed. "Very well. But I am taking
you under duress. I do not think it wise."

"We stick together," Felicity reiterated.

With Peter straddling the saddle in front of her,
they rode side by side to the hill due west of the one
on which Kilraven was camped. Well below the
crown they dismounted and climbed the rest of the
way on foot, flattening when they reached the top.
The hill they were on was higher than the other one.
Peter giggled as they crawled to a spot where they
could look down on the encampment. "This is fun,
Ma." Then his grin faded. "Look! They're hurting
Zach?"

Felicity shifted so she was in front of him, and he
could not see what was taking place. Shock settled
in as she watched the horrid spectacle. Out of the
corner of her eye she noticed Peter open his mouth
as if to cry out, and she quickly covered it with her
hand. "We can't let them hear us, son" she whispered into his ear.

Simon wanted to look away but could not bring
himself to do so. Zach was their friend. Zach was
trying to help them. And there he was, strung between posts, being whipped by Lord Kilraven. Each
stroke of the lash made Simon flinch as if he were
the one being whipped. Zach never once cried out.
That amazed Simon. Had it been him, he would

have screamed himself hoarse. But Zach took it, and while his body arched and he thrashed wildly, he never gave voice to the torment Simon was sure he was feeling.

Felicity looked, turned away, and looked again. She never expected anything like this. Zach had fought the Blackfeet, the Sioux, even the Apaches once. She had assumed he would get the best of Kilraven's party as he had bested all his other enemies. After a while she could not watch any more. How he took it, she would never know.

"The whipping is over," Simon said softly. He had seldom been so glad of anything. He saw Kilraven and some of the others smile and laugh as they turned their backs on the blood-streaked figure. Zach appeared to be barely conscious.

"Are they just going to let him hang there?"

"Looks like," Simon said.

"That's inhuman," Felicity declared. "What do we do? We have to help him. We have to do something."

Simon nodded. "The trick is to do it without getting ourselves killed. Make no mistake. Kilraven is no longer content with driving us from our home. He wants us dead."

"What makes you say that?"

"Call it an educated guess." Simon drew back from the edge and she followed suit. "I'll be careful when I go down there. But if anything happens to me, go to Bent's Fort. Someone there will get word to Nate King."

"When *you* go down there?" Felicity said.

"We can't take Peter with us, and we certainly can't leave him alone," Simon said. "Who knows what might happen by. Another wolf, a mountain lion, a bear, you name it."

"We could both ride to Bent's Fort and send word to Nate," Felicity proposed.

"It could take weeks to find him. By then Zach will be long dead."

"Maybe we can persuade St. Vrain to send men to help Zach."

"Even that would take too long." Simon refused to abandon Zach to Kilraven's cruelties. "And there's no guarantee anyone except St. Vrain would come. Zach is not as well liked as his sire." The truth was, a lot of those who frequented the trading post would like nothing better than to have Zach dead. Some, because he was a half-breed. Some, because Zach had a knack for making enemies. "I have to do this myself."

Dread clawing at her vitals, Felicity asked, "When do you propose to sneak down there?"

Simon squinted skyward. "As soon as the sun goes down." He did not look forward to it. He was no fighter, like Zach. He was a homesteader, plain and simple, and would as soon live the rest of his days without ever lifting a finger against his fellow man. But that was not realistic. On the frontier, conflicts were part and parcel of everyday life. It was a risk every homesteader had to brave daily, and part of the reason more people had not flocked West yet. But they would. Simon was confident that one day the prairie and the foothills and the mountains would teem with towns and cities and farms like his own. He looked forward to that day. He longed for it.

Felicity stared at the slumped figure between the posts. She knew her husband was right; he had to go help Zach. But her love for him made her desperate for an alternative. "What will you do when you get there? What help can you be when there are so many of them?"

"I will do what I can," Simon said. He had no plan other than to free Zach.

"If Peter and I went with you, we could watch your back. You don't have eyes in the back of your head, you know."

"I appreciate your devotion, but no. You will wait up here, and if the worst comes to pass, do as we discussed."

"Is that an order?" Felicity did not like being told what to do. She never had, even as a little girl. One of the things she admired the most about Simon was that he was not the bossy sort. He was not one of those husbands always commanding their wives to do this or that. He valued her opinions and sentiments, always gave her a say in all they did.

"Don't start," Simon said.

Felicity sulked the rest of the afternoon. She racked her mind for an argument that would convince him to change his mind, but there was none. Not with Peter to think of. One of them had to look after their son, and in this particular instance it had to be her.

Gradually the sun dipped toward the horizon. Felicity marked its descent with mounting trepidation. When it began to sink bit by bit, her anxiety climbed in corresponding degrees.

Simon was studying the camp below. He had

memorized where the fires were and where the horse string was in relation to the fires and where the sentries were posted.

Earlier, about four in the afternoon, a party of men had ridden off into the valley, leading a string of horses. They returned about six, and Simon was surprised to see long poles lashed to the horses. Trimmed saplings, he suspected, which were then used to erect makeshift tents out of spare blankets. There was one tent for Lord Kilraven and his wife; another for his niece, Cadena; and a third, much smaller, for the maids.

The shadows lengthened. Twilight descended, and was in turn eclipsed by the starry mantle of night.

Simon stirred and turned. "It's time," he announced.

Felicity embraced him. There was so much she wanted to say, but the lump in her throat made it difficult to speak. Finally she whispered, "Come back to me. My life would be empty without you."

They turned to Peter, who had fallen asleep curled in a ball with his arm for a pillow.

Simon tenderly touched his son's cheek. "No matter what, don't let anything happen to him." He looked Felicity in the eyes, and when she nodded, he kissed her. "I love you."

"And I you."

Simon rose and headed down the hill.

Chapter Sixteen

The cool of night revived Zach. From off the high peaks came a brisk breeze to dispel the heat of the day. He was startled awake by what he took to be the feel of clammy fingers running along the blood-seeped furrows that crisscrossed his back from his shoulders to his waist. His arms throbbed with pain, his shoulders screamed for relief. He tried to lick his lips, but his mouth was as dry as a desert.

Zach gazed about him. Kilraven's party ringed half a dozen campfires. At the nearest sat his lordship and Lady Kilraven, servants at their elbow ready to wait on every whim. Hatred welled inside him, hatred so strong he had to take deep breaths to calm himself.

To relieve cramps in his arms, Zach tried to flex them. The slight movement provoked extreme torture. His wrists were rubbed raw of skin; the ropes had eaten into his flesh and were caked with dry blood.

Zach let his chin droop. He was nearly spent. The whippings had taken more out of him than he would have imagined possible. But he refused to succumb and pass out again. His father liked to say that so long as there was life, there was hope. In Zach's case, so long as there was life, he had a chance at exacting revenge.

"Look who is back among the living."

Zach glanced up. Cadena had come over. She was smiling and sipping from a china cup. He did not reply.

"I must say, I admire your stamina. Most men would be at death's doorstep after two whippings."

Zach glared at her.

"Nothing to say? Or is that you can't? Would you care for a drink? You must be terribly thirsty after hanging there most of the day without water."

Against his better judgment, Zach was able to rasp out, "I would like some water, yes."

"Too bad," Cadena smirked. She drained her cup and smacked her lips. "Delicious, this tea. You should try some."

"None of you will ever see your own country again," Zach told her.

"Oh my. Is this where I faint in fear?" Cadena laughed. "I expect better of you than idle threats."

Zach bowed his head. He had said all he was going to.

"My uncle has given word that you are not to be given any sustenance whatsoever," Cadena informed him. "No water, no food, nothing. In the morning, if you are still alive, and it certainly seems you will be, he plans to whip you again and go on whipping you until his lash bites clear down to the bone. By this time tomorrow night you will be . . ." She paused. "What is that quaint expression I heard at Bent's Fort? Oh, yes. You will be worm food."

Zach closed his eyes. He must conserve his strength, his energy.

"Say something," Cadena said, and when he didn't, she stamped her foot in that habit she had. "Come now. This is childish. I came over to talk to you, thinking you might like the company."

Now it was Zach who smirked at her. He could not resist. "I generally shy away from the company of bitches."

Cadena's features might have been carved from ice. "Very well. Have it your way. Be petty if you want. But I will tell you this." She took a step nearer. "When you have breathed your last, I am going to treat myself to a glass of wine to celebrate your passing." Pivoting on a heel, she walked off.

Zach laughed. It came out as more of a bray but it felt good, damn good.

"You are in awful good spirits for someone who won't ever set eyes on his wife and kin again."

From around the post on the right strolled Edwin Ryker, his rifle in the crook of his elbow. He had a piece of roast venison impaled on the tip of his knife.

"Come to gloat?"

"I brought you this," Ryker said, and wagged his knife.

"I thought no one is to feed me?" Zach said. "I thought you needed Kilraven's permission to talk to me."

"No one tells me what to do." Ryker gazed after the retreating figure of Cadena. "What did she want?"

"To show me she is no different from her uncle."

Ryker sighed. "No, she isn't. She had me thinking she was for a spell, but I came to my senses. To hell with her, and to hell with him."

To Zach's astonishment, the meat was suddenly at his mouth.

"Here. Eat as much as you want."

The aroma was more than Zach could endure. He sank his teeth into the succulent deer meat and chewed lustily. Seldom had venison tasted so delicious. He swallowed it after only a few chews and bit off another piece.

"Slow down there, hoss. You'll make yourself sick," Ryker cautioned.

Zach stopped chewing long enough to ask, "Why are you doing this?"

Ryker glanced toward where Kilraven and Saxona were having an animated talk with Cadena. "Think of it as my way of mending fences. I never counted on anything like this."

"If it's forgiveness you're after, you've come to the wrong person," Zach said bluntly, and took another bite.

"Hell, give me more credit. I know you well enough to know that if you had a pistol in your hand right now, you'd shoot me dead." Ryker, strangely enough, smiled. "I also know that your pa is a man of honor, and I'm hoping some of that rubbed off on you."

"I've lost your trail," Zach confessed between chews.

Again Ryker glanced at the Kilravens. "I need to

talk fast. They might spot me." He stood so his back was to them. "It's like this. I want nothing more to do with that bastard. He went back on his word to me, which frees me to go back on my word to him. I aim to light a shuck here in a bit, and good riddance."

"You're leaving?"

"I should say I am. I'm heading for Bent's Fort. After that, who knows? I've been meaning to pay Oregon Country a visit, and now is as good a time as any." Ryker grinned. "If you want me, you will have to come a far piece to find me. I am gambling it will be too much bother."

"If you really want to make amends, cut me loose," Zach said. He bit off yet another morsel.

"Sorry. I don't trust you. I wouldn't put it past you to try to kill me." Ryker lowered his voice. "But I have done you one other favor. I got hold of your weapons. They are wrapped in a blanket over by the horse string. If you can get loose, my advice is take them and get the hell out of here."

Zach glanced toward the string. "I don't see a blanket."

"It's there. Your ammo pouch and possibles bag and the rest, too." Ryker stepped back and lowered his knife. "It is the best I can do, King. If it's not enough, I've told you where you can find me." He turned to go.

"Do me one more favor, and I'll consider not looking you up," Zach said.

Ryker paused in midstride. "Depends on the favor. I've already told you I won't cut you loose."

"That's not it. I want you to promise me that you'll never mention Kilraven or his people to anyone.

Never say a word about him hiring you or what went on here."

Ryker's brow puckered. "As favors go it is peculiar. I trust you have a good reason?"

"Your word," Zach said.

"If you give me yours that we're even, and that I won't have to spend the rest of my life looking over my shoulder."

"Consider it given," Zach said.

"That's not good enough. I want to hear it, straight tongue."

Zach hesitated, but only for a few seconds. "I swear by my wife, I swear by my mother and my father, I swear by my sister, that I will not hunt you down and kill you. Will that do?"

"That'll do fine." Ryker raised a finger to his hat. "Good luck."

Zach noticed Lord Kilraven staring at them. He sagged to give the impression he was on the verge of collapse, when actually, thanks to the venison, a newfound surge of vitality coursed through his veins. He wished there had been more meat. The scant amount he ate had done wonders. But the effect might not last long.

Footsteps warned Zach someone else was approaching. He could guess who it was.

"Confound that man, he never does as I command. His impertinence is galling. What did he say to you?"

"He was poking fun," Zach lied. "Get in your own licks while you still can."

"What is that supposed to mean?" Lord Kilraven demanded.

"If you were smart you would finish me off now, but you are not smart so you won't."

Lord Kilraven chortled. "Let me be sure I understand the extent of your stupidity. You *want* me to kill you here and now?"

"You would if you had a lick of sense."

"Fascinating," Kilraven said. "But I would rather we end this in the morning. That'll give you all night to think about it, to worry, to weep with anxiety if you want."

"You have me confused with one of the women," Zach said flatly. "I would never cry over something as trivial as this."

"Trivial?" Lord Kilraven repeated. "Your own death? Has your mind snapped from the punishment I inflicted?"

"Everyone dies. You. Me. Everyone," Zach told him. "To die is the natural course of things. We all end the same, rich or poor, powerful or run of the mill. In the scheme of life, dying is nothing special."

Kilraven laughed. "Your homespun philosophy amuses me. But I can assure you that you will not think your death so inconsequential come morning. You will cherish life to the last. You will cling to it as a mother to her precious newborn."

"What would you know of mothers?" Zach countered. "Your wife mentioned that you don't have any kids. That's why you let your niece traipse all over creation with you."

"No, we do not, but it is not for a lack of trying," Lord Kilraven said curtly. "And it is hardly a subject worthy of discussion with the likes of you."

"There is a saying in these parts," Zach said.

"There is no fool like someone who does not know they are a fool."

"Yet more cryptic nonsense. Very well. Have your fun while you may, for tomorrow it ends forever."

Zach gazed about the encampment. "You might consider sending your servants back to Bent's Fort."

"Whatever for?"

"Tell them that if you haven't shown up in a couple of weeks, they should go back to Britain."

"Your bluster begins to bore me," Lord Kilraven said sharply. "Do you honestly expect me to deprive myself of their services? To dress myself? To cook my own food?"

"Do they wash you, too?"

"Go ahead. Scoff. Your envy falls on deaf ears. My station in life entitles me to pamper myself, and pamper myself I will."

"If any of them are alive after this is over, maybe they will bury you, too," Zach said.

Kilraven's disgust was transparent. "Infantile, is what you are. Our discussion is at an end."

Zach spent the next several hours in a state of anxious expectation. He could not try to free himself until most everyone was asleep, and no one showed an inclination to turn in.

Along about ten, Severn and Meldon checked that the ropes securing his wrists to the post were still knotted and tight. Smiling maliciously, Severn gave each rope a tug, fully aware of the pain it would cause.

"This one's not going anywhere."

"I'm looking forward to tomorrow," Meldon remarked. "I've never seen anyone whipped to death before. It will be something to talk about when we get back."

"You'll never see England again," Zach informed them.

Severn scowled. "You need to learn to mind your betters, boy." With that, he drove his knee up and in.

The pain that exploded in Zach's groin nearly blacked him out. All his newfound vitality evaporated. His legs buckled and he hung by his wrists, the night swimming around him.

"Better be careful," Meldon said to Severn. "His lordship won't like it if you deprive him of his entertainment."

"I never yet heard of a good one to the bollocks killing a man," Severn responded. "Think of it as a little something for this sod to remember us by."

Between clenched teeth Zach hissed, "I will remember you were a fool, and that is all."

"Make me madder, why don't you?" Severn gripped Zach's hair and gave his head a violent wrench. "You don't know when to leave well alone. But you won't be acting so tough after his lordship is done with you." He spat in Zach's face.

Zach nearly went berserk. Every instinct he possessed cried for him to kick, to bite, to strike out in any way possible. It took all the self-control he had not to.

Laughing, Severn and Meldon strutted toward a fire.

Time passed. The Kilravens, their niece, and the maids retired to their respective tents. Everyone except the sentries turned in. The constellations crawled across the night sky, and by their positions it was pressing two in the morning and Zach was twisting and turning his wrists in a determined bid to gain his freedom, when a hand touched his arm.

"It's me," Simon Ward whispered. "Don't move. I'll cut you free."

Zach checked on the sentries. None were looking in his direction. The instant the ropes were severed, he started to lower his arms and immediately regretted it. Sheer anguish spiked along both arms to his shoulders.

"Are you all right?" Simon whispered.

"Worry about them, if you must worry about anyone," Zach whispered, and motioned with a sweep of his head at the sleepers. "They are all going to die."

Chapter Seventeen

Felicity Ward paced back and forth. She was too worried, too upset, to stay still. Simon had been gone much longer than she thought he would. She had seen no trace of him since dark fell, not so much as a glimpse, and she had strained her eyes until they ached.

Peter was asleep in her arms. It was the middle of the night, and stars sparkled in the firmament. From out of the inky veil of the wilderness came constant cries and shrieks and howls and occasional roars. The meat eaters were abroad, filling the air with their bedlam and the distress of their prey.

Twice Felicity had heard growls much too near the hill. She imagined a mountain lion or some other predator stalking them or their horses, and the dark became alive with moving shadows. Shadows that might only be her imagination. She could not say for sure, and that was the worst part. The uncertainty. Dreading a snarl and a rush that never came. Her nerves were frayed. She was a wreck.

So when Felicity heard something coming up the hill toward her, heard it breathing heavily and the patter of what she took to be heavy paws, she whirled, and raised her club, the only weapon she had, and a pitiful defense against fangs and claws.

Felicity steeled herself to go down fighting. She would protect Peter with her dying breath; if she had to, she would sacrifice herself to save him. Love for him filled her heart to near bursting, and she planted herself in grim resolve.

A shape heaved out of the night. It stopped, and gasping for breath, wheezed, "Felicity? What are you doing?"

Tears moistening her eyes, Felicity threw herself at Simon. She almost forgot about Peter, almost crushed him between them. She had to settle for dropping the club and wrapping her free arm around Simon's neck and carefully pulling him close. "Thank you, God," she breathed in his ear. "Thank you, thank you, thank you."

"I'm worn out from running," Simon said. "Zach said we must hurry."

Felicity looked past him. "Where is he? Weren't you able to free him?"

"I cut him loose," Simon said, "and we snuck out of their camp. Then he had me wait while he snuck back in and got me these."

It was then that Felicity realized he had pistols wedged under his belt and was holding two rifles. "But where is Zach? Why isn't he with you?"

"He wouldn't come," Simon revealed. "He's going to, and I quote, 'make war.'"

"But he is one and they are many."

"I pointed that out to him but he says it doesn't matter. After what they did to him, he intends to count coup until they are all dead, or he is." Simon handed her a rifle.

"This is awful."

"I suppose I can't blame him," Simon said. "You should have seen his back. The scourging, what it did to him. I don't think I could have taken it." He shuddered. "Zach will have scars for the rest of his life."

"I could tend his wounds," Felicity said, and stared forlornly down into the dark.

"We must leave," Simon said. "Zach wants us to head for the cabin, lock ourselves in, and stay there until we hear from him. If he doesn't show up in ten days we are to go to Bent's Fort and get word to his father."

"Ten days?" Felicity said. "Why so long?"

Simon gazed at the crown of the flat-topped hill. "I don't know. He refused to tell me what he's up to." Simon frowned. "God, how I wish Nate were here. He's the only one who could stop Zach from doing something he might regret later on."

"I don't like the idea of riding off and leaving him." Felicity would rather stay where they were and await developments.

"Zach says if we don't, we are at risk," Simon relayed. "I don't like it any better than you, but we will do as he wants. I trust him. For all his wildness, for all his savagery, he is our friend. Our true and dear friend."

"What about our other horses?"

"We will fetch them. He instructed us to give Kilraven's camp a wide berth and make a beeline for home. He was quite insistent we swing to the south and not the north."

"Why?" Felicity regarded the flickering campfires. All was still and quiet, or appeared to be.

"I asked Zach and all he did was smile. A smile that chilled me to the bone," Simon said. "I almost feel sorry for them. Almost," he repeated softly.

"I feel sorry for Zach," Felicity said. "He has taken so many lives already. How can his soul bear the burden of taking more?"

"He is a warrior. That is what warriors do."

"But it still has to have some effect. There must come a time when every warrior feels regret."

"Not Zach."

"What does he feel, then?" Felicity asked.

Simon did not reply.

Cadena Taylor was sleeping peacefully when a hand was clamped over her mouth. She awoke with a start and started to sit up. Then the tip of a sharp blade was pressed against her throat just hard enough to break the skin, and Cadena froze.

Lips brushed her ear.

"Make a sound and I'll slit your throat."

Cadena gulped. She was bodily lifted and hauled to the back of her makeshift tent. The blanket had been cut from about waist height to the bottom. She was forced to get down on all fours and crawl through, the knife always at her neck. Once out, she was yanked to her feet and propelled around the perimeter of the camp to where several horses were saddled and waiting. Along the way they passed a slain sentry. He lay on his back, his limbs askew, his head hanging at an unnatural angle. Her stomach did flip-flops and she smothered a whimper.

Near the horses lay another body. Or so Cadena thought until she was roughly shoved to her knees. She was shocked to discover Lady Kilraven, bound and gagged.

Zach King squatted in front of her. He had found a brown shirt somewhere, and it was partially buttoned. He also had his weapons, all of them, including his bowie and his tomahawk. He did not say anything as he began to tie her wrists in front of her.

Cadena opened her mouth to say something. The instant she did, he looked at her. He just looked, but something in his gaze, in the set of his features, stilled her tongue. She had never seen anyone look at her in quite that way. It scared her. She remained docile as she was gagged and then swung onto one of the horses. A lead rope was looped about its neck, and the neck of another horse. Onto that one Lady Kilraven was thrown and tied down so she would not fall off. From the way she sagged when he picked her up, Cadena knew Saxona was unconscious.

Zach climbed onto his sorrel, took the end of the lead rope, and jabbed his heels. Shifting in the saddle, he watched behind them. There were no outcries. No shots rang out. Soon they were at the bottom of the hill, and once there, out of earshot of the camp, Zach rode faster.

Fear gnawed at Cadena like so many ravening
ants. She was being abducted yet again! Part of her
refused to believe this was happening. Part of her insisted she must be dreaming. But the thud of hooves,
the creak of the saddle under her, the wind in her
hair, the pain in her wrists and the uncomfortable
gag in her mouth, were proof it was all too real.

Cadena was a terrible judge of distances. They
might have gone half a mile or less when they came
to another hill and climbed to its bare summit. She
was surprised when Zach stopped and climbed
down, even more surprised when he came over and
removed the gag from her mouth. Lady Kilraven
was a limp bundle of white.

"May I speak?" Cadena asked.

"So long as you do it quietly."

"What have you done to my aunt?"

Zach patted his tomahawk. "A rap on the noggin
with this. Not with the edge, though. I don't want
her dead. I don't want either of you dead."

"Then why take us?" Cadena wanted to know.

"To use as bait."

Cadena did not like the sound of that. She liked it
even less that he was in no hurry to go anywhere.
He pulled her off her horse and roughly sat her
down, then did the same with Lady Kilraven, leaving her sprawled on her back. "How did you get
free? How did you saddle those horses without anyone noticing?"

"Dead sentries can't notice much."

Cadena thought of the one she had seen, his head
nearly severed. "How many of them did you kill?"

Zach looked at her in that way again.

"All of them? Dear God." Cadena was trying to put on a brave show, but she was more scared than she had ever been in her entire life. She was in the clutches of a savage with no regard for human life. "You want my uncle to come after you? Is that what this is about? You intend to lure him into the mountains. But what good will it do you? You are still greatly outnumbered."

Zach King said a strange thing. "You would think so, wouldn't you?"

Severn could not say what awakened him. He lay in the dark listening but heard only snores and the wind and the distant bark of coyotes. He closed his eyes to go back to sleep and then snapped them open again. It was dark, completely dark, and it shouldn't be. The sentries were supposed to keep the campfires going all night.

Severn sat up, his blanket falling around his waist. The fire nearest to him had gone out. Of the other fires, only two feebly glowed. He pushed to his feet, mad enough to cudgel someone. "If his lordship finds out, there will be hell to pay," he said to himself.

Gathering up his pistols and rifle, Severn stalked to the east side of the hill. A sentry was supposed to be roving back and forth at all times, but there was no sign of him. "Owen?" he called, but not too loudly. "Where the bloody hell are you?"

When there was no response, Severn conducted a hurried search. He had gone a short way when his foot bumped something in his path. Glancing down, he was dumfounded to behold a prone form.

"Who—?" Severn began. Then he saw the face bathed by pale starlight, saw that the head was connected by only a few shreds of flesh.

The contents of Severn's stomach tried to come out his mouth. Swallowing bitter bile, he turned away. "Who could have done this?" The explanation hit him with the force of a thunderclap. "Hostiles!" he blurted, and sped toward the blanket tents to warn his lordship.

That was when Severn saw the posts. He ran over and gaped at the dangling ropes. Examining one, he swore. They had been cut. Hostiles were not to blame for the sentry. "It was the half-breed!" Severn exclaimed. Bringing up his rifle, he spun in a circle, but all he saw were sleeping figures and picketed horses.

In swift order, Severn woke up Bromley, Meldon, and York. He had Bromley and Meldon go check on the other sentries while he and York hurried from fire to fire, stirring the embers and adding firewood. In short order the encampment was again lit from end to end.

Severn was making for the tents when the other three fell into step on either side of him. "Well?"

"Dead," Bromley reported. "All the sentries are dead."

"How could he kill them *all*?" Meldon marveled. "Without making a sound? I couldn't do that. Could you do that?"

"Four horses are missing," Bromley reported. "That's not all. We made a head count, as you wanted. Our guide is missing."

"Edwin Ryker?" Severn stopped in midstride.

"Did you find blood on his blankets? Or signs of a struggle?"

Bromley shook his head. "You don't understand. He and all his possessions are gone. His blankets, his saddle, everything, and his horse is one of those missing."

"Are you suggesting he rode off on his own? That he deserted us?"

"So it would seem," Bromley said. "Unless he has joined forces with Zach King, which I can't see happening."

"Neither can I," Severn agreed, hastening on to the blanket tents. He halted in front of the largest and cleared his throat. "Your lordship? I apologize for disturbing you at this hour, but we have a problem on our hands."

Rustling came from within. "What was that?" their lord and master's sleepy voice demanded.

"We have a problem," Severn said. "A serious problem."

It was half a minute before the blankets parted. His white hair disheveled, Kilraven fumbled with the belt to his robe. "Explain yourselves," he demanded. "Keep it succinct. And it had better be as serious as you claim it to be or you will rue waking me."

Severn detailed all they knew, ending with, "What would you have us do? We are at your command."

"Of course you are." Kilraven ran a hand through his hair. "Wake everyone. Have the cook make breakfast. If he grumbles it is too early, remind him it is a long walk and an even longer swim back to England. I will be out directly after I am dressed."

The blankets closed and Severn and the others turned to do as they had been bid. But they had barely taken three steps when the blankets were snapped apart again.

"Where is my wife? Where is Saxona?"

"Sir?" Severn said.

Bromley gestured. "We have not seen any sign of her, your lordship. We assumed she was with you."

"Scour the camp," Kilraven barked. "If anything has happened to her—" He did not finish and went back in.

Severn stepped to a smaller tent and coughed a few times to be polite. "Miss Taylor? Your uncle wants everyone up. There has been murder most foul, and the breed is on the loose." He waited, and when he received no acknowledgment, he repeated himself, only louder. More silence ensued. He made bold to poke his head inside, and swore.

Lord Kilraven did not take the news well. He did not take it well at all. He stormed about the camp, making sure everyone was up and dressed and ready to head out at dawn. "We will find my wife and my niece, however long it takes!" he raged as the sky began to brighten. "We will chase Zach King to the ends of the earth if need be!"

Severn happened to be gazing to the northwest a few minutes later and could not quite credit his eyes. He hastened to his lordship. "The breed is a lot closer than we thought, your lordship."

Kilraven gazed where Severn pointed.

On the crown of a nearby hill, mounted and holding the lead rope to two horses on which Lady Kilraven and Cadena were perched, was Zach King. As they sat eyes on his, he raised an arm and beckoned.

"I'll be damned," Lord Kilraven growled, and grimly smiled. "Everyone mount up. His arrogance will be the death of him."

Chapter Eighteen

So far Zach's plan was working.

Two days had gone by. Two days of hard riding steadily northwest. Two days of winding deeper, ever deeper, into the Rockies.

Zach knew the country well. He had hunted it many a time with his father and Shakespeare McNair when he was young, and he had passed through it again on his way to Bent's Fort to buy the supplies and perfume. At the last moment he had decided to visit the Wards. It was well he did.

The lead rope wrapped tight in his hand, Zach drew rein high on a switchback. His sorrel was winded. So were the other horses. Not quite a mile below were his pursuers. Each day he had gained a little more ground on them, until now he felt safe in announcing, "We will rest for a spell."

"Thank God!" Saxona Kilraven declared.

The chase had been rough on the women. Neither were skilled riders. Most of their journey west from

St. Louis had been spent on the seat of a rolling wagon. They were a mess. Their hair was bedraggled, their loose-fitting white cotton nightgowns were speckled with dust and smeared with grass stains and dirt from sleeping on the ground. Their eyes were bloodshot and puffy and had dark shadows under them.

"Can we please eat something?" Cadena requested. "I am famished."

"We will eat when we stop for the night," Zach told her. "As we have done all along."

Lady Kilraven adopted a haughty expression. "One meal a day, and that consists of water and that abominable salted meat you frontier types are so absurdly fond of."

"The salted meat is called jerky," Zach said. "My wife made it herself."

"I don't care what it is called or who made it," Lady Kilraven retorted. "It tastes wretched. Admit it. You are trying to starve us to death."

"You are no use to me dead." Zach dismounted and crooked a finger at them. "Climb down and stretch your legs. We won't be here long."

Cadena held out her bound wrists. "You could at least be a gentleman and help us."

"You're not helpless."

Lady Kilraven uttered a grunt of contempt as she slid off and took a few shuffling steps. "Every muscle in my body aches, my legs worst of all. I will not be able to walk for a month after this."

Zach marked the progress of their would-be rescuers. Every last member of Lord Kilraven's party was after them, including the other two women, the maids, who rode at the end of the long line, with the pack animals. He was sorry they were along, but he had his mind made up.

"What do you hope to accomplish by this lunacy?" Lady Kilraven demanded. "My husband will never give up, not so long as breath remains in his body."

"I am counting on that," Zach said.

"To what end? Do you intend to pick him off with your rifle? Killing him will not change anything. I will have the hunting preserve built to spite you."

"You take a lot for granted."

"Spare us your idle threats. If you were going to harm Cadena and me, you would have done so by now."

Zach almost regretted what he had in store for them. Almost. He let them rest for five minutes; then it was back in the saddle. Another hour of difficult riding, of more steep slopes choked with timber, brought them to the spot he had been making for all long.

It was a high country park, as the mountain men called them, a grassy vale half a mile broad, replete with wildflowers, situated between two ridges. Zach cantered to the center, leading the women. "This is as far as we go," he revealed as he drew rein. "Off your horses."

"Another rest so soon after the last?" Lady Kilraven said. "Have you a kernel of compassion in that heathen body, after all?"

"You are a fine one to talk about compassion, lady," Zach criticized, "after what you and your husband wanted to do to the Wards."

"Oh, please," Saxona said. "The strong have always lorded it over the weak. It is the nature of things."

"Remember you said that in an hour or so."

"What do you mean?"

Zach fixed his attention on the ridge they had crossed to reach the park. He figured it would be a quarter of an hour before Lord Kilraven reached it.

Both women were regarding him in puzzlement.

"What are you up to?" Cadena asked. "Why are we just waiting here? Do you want them to catch up?"

Zach went on watching the ridge.

"You could at least have the decency to answer her," Lady Kilraven complained. "I don't understand, either. You stole us from our camp. You brought us all this way. And now what? Is it your intention to slit our throats and leave our bodies for my husband to find?"

"I don't make it a habit to kill women," Zach said dryly. "But if you are that set on having your throat slit, I might be able to oblige you."

"You make no sense," Lady Kilraven declared.

"The strong over the weak, remember?" Zach reminded her.

The two women moved off a few yards and whispered. In a short while they were back, and they were plainly worried.

"I agree with my niece," Lady Kilraven said. "You are up to something. I would very much like to know what it is."

"Get used to disappointment." Zach looked at them and experienced a twinge of conscience. "Is there any chance you could persuade your husband to forget about his hunting preserve and head back to England?"

Saxona's mouth curled in a sneer. "I wouldn't try, even if I thought he would listen to me."

"That's too bad." Zach steeled himself for what he had to do. "You have called the thunder and lightning down on your heads. I wash my hands of the whole lot of you."

"Whatever are you talking about?"

Zach tensed. Several riders had appeared. Severn and some others. He quickly climbed back on the sorrel and snagged the lead rope. "Your rescuers will be here shortly, ladies. You might not believe this, but I wish there had been another way."

"Wait. You are leaving us here?" Lady Kilraven said.

"And taking our horses?" From Cadena.

A jab of Zach's heels brought the sorrel to a trot. He crossed the park to the ridge to the north and reached the top about the same time that Severn and the advance riders descended to the park.

The rest of Lord Kilraven's party were just coming over the south ridge.

Lady Kilraven and Cadena waved their bounds arms and excitedly hopped up and down.

Zach galloped on. If he had calculated correctly, he would strike the trail he wanted in short order. He had allowed for how much distance those he sought had traveled since he struck their trail the first time on the way to the Wards. It was a gamble, this ploy of his, but if it worked, the Wards were free to go on living in their valley for as long as they desired.

Fortune favored him. Zach rode for ten minutes when he came on a wide swath of ground churned by scores of hooves. Reining up, he jumped down and examined the tracks. Those he sought had passed that way less than an hour before.

Zach climbed on the sorrel and followed the churned swath. Speed was called for. He had no way of knowing how long he had. The Kilravens might make camp at the park or they might turn around and head right back.

Fully aware of the peril he courted, Zach pressed on until he spotted the ones he was after. Their backs were to him. They had no idea he was there. He remedied that. Reining to a halt, he whooped and hollered and screeched. Predictably, they wheeled their mounts and gazed in bewilderment.

Zach gave them extra incentive. He whipped his rifle to his shoulder and fired over their heads. Then, laughing, he dropped the lead rope, hauled on the sorrel's reins, and raced back the way he had come.

They raced after him.

Zach figured that by leaving the extra horses, he bought himself the minute or so it would take for those who were after him to snatch the horses. A minute might not sound like much, but it could make all the difference.

Now all he had to do was stay alive.

Lord Kilraven permitted his wife to embrace him, albeit briefly. Drawing away, he thoughtfully regarded both her and his niece. "You say he just rode off and left you?"

Saxona nodded. "His behavior is most inexplicable. But what else are we to expect from these provincials? And a savage, no less."

"He is half-white," Cadena said.

Lady Kilraven sniffed. "You will find, my dear, that when the lower and higher natures are mixed, the lower nature often prevails over the higher by virtue of its base tendencies."

"He just rode off and left you?" Lord Kilraven said again, and turned to Severn and Bromley. "What do you two make of it? Deuced peculiar that he brought them all this way for no reason."

"Maybe he wanted to draw us away from the Wards," Bromley speculated.

"I could not begin to guess, your lordship," Severn said. "Do you want me to take some of the men and go after him?"

"No. I want a fire, and tea brewed for the ladies. After they are refreshed and rested, we will start back," Lord Kilraven directed. "We will go straightaway to the Wards' homestead and appropriate it as our own. I am through coddling these colonials."

"As you wish, sir," Severn said, and turned to relay the orders. Movement on the ridge to the north gave him pause. "Bloody hell!" he exclaimed before he could catch himself. "It's him!"

They all looked. They all saw Zach King come riding down the north ridge as if the demons of hell were on his heels.

"What in God's name does he think he is doing?" Bromley asked in amazement.

"*He* is attacking *us!*" Saxona marveled.

Severn whipped his rifle up. "As soon as he reaches the bottom I will drop him."

Their wonderment grew when Zach, midway down the slope, reined to the east and shouted something. The same words, over and over.

"What is he saying?" Lord Kilraven asked. "I can't quite make it out."

"He is insane," Saxona said. "There is no other explanation."

Cadena took a few steps, her head cocked. "I think I can make it out." She listened intently, then blanched. "No! Surely not! We heard about them at the trading post. They are the worst of the lot."

"What are you on about?" Lord Kilraven impatiently snipped.

"Can't you hear yet what he is shouting?"

"Enlighten us, if you please."

Cadena raised her voice in imitation of Zach King. "The Blackfeet are coming! The Blackfeet are coming!"

The next instant a swarm of riders swept over the top of the north ridge. Painted warriors astride painted war horses.

Saxona's hand flew to her throat. "Merciful heaven! There must be a hundred of those devils!"

The warriors had seen them. War whoops rent the air as they hurtled toward the park.

"Oh God, oh God, oh God, oh God."

Simon was feeding the chickens when the horseman appeared. He ran to the cabin to warn Felicity, then ran back out with his rifle. She emerged holding Peter and a pistol.

"Can you tell who it is?"

"Not yet." Shielding his eyes from the sun's glare,

Simon fought down rising apprehension. Soon he smiled and declared, "It's Zach! He made it back safely!"

"I'll fix coffee."

Simon stayed outside. He noticed that Zach was slumped in the saddle. Fatigue, Simon thought, and then Zach reined to a halt and glanced up. "My word!" Simon took a step back. "Are you all right?"

"I am in one piece," Zach answered, drawing rein. His features were haggard, suggesting he had not slept in days.

"Where is Lord Kilraven? Should we get ready to leave for Bent's Fort?"

"No."

Felicity came back out. She was smiling but her smile died when she saw Zach. She hurried to her husband's side. "What have I missed? What has he told you?"

"Nothing," Simon said.

Zach gazed at their cabin, at the stable, at the chicken coop. "You have a nice place here."

Simon and Felicity looked at one another.

"This is your home," Zach had gone on. "No one has the right to take another man's home. I hope when your son grows up that he appreciates the price you had to pay."

Felicity walked over and put her hand on his leg. "Zach? Where is Lord Kilraven?"

"Gone."

"Gone as in he gave up and left? Or gone as in dead?"

Zach did not respond.

"What about Lady Kilraven?" Felicity asked. "And Cadena and all the rest? Where are they?"

"Gone."

"Please, Zach," Felicity said. "We need to know more. I want to hear all of it."

"All of it?" Zach said. "Imagine—," he paused, and glanced at her, and swallowed. "No. Don't imagine it. There is gone, and there is *gone*."

"Are you saying they are dead?" Simon asked. "By whose hand? Surely you did not slay all of them yourself?"

"They met up with a war party," Zach explained, and let it go at that.

"Which tribe?" Simon pressed him.

"I'd rather not say."

Felicity was thinking of Saxona and Cadena and the maids. "Are the women dead, too?"

"They were spared, except for Lady Kilraven. None of the warriors wanted her."

"Come inside," Felicity urged. "You need to get some food into you."

"I need to forget, is what I need." Zach raised the sorrel's reins. "I'll be on my way. I have perfume to buy."

"We can't thank you enough for helping us," Simon said sincerely. "I mean that from the bottom of my heart."

Zach King managed a smile. "What are friends for?"

NIGHT HAWK

STEPHEN OVERHOLSER

He came to the ranch with a mile-wide chip on his shoulder and no experience whatsoever. But it was either work on the Circle L or rot in jail, and he figured even the toughest labor was better than a life behind bars. He's got a lot to learn though, and he'd better learn it fast because he's about to face one of the toughest cattle drives in the country. They've got an ornery herd, not much water and danger everywhere they look. The greenhorn the cowboys call Night Hawk may not know much, but he does know this: The smallest mistake could cost him his life.

ISBN 10: 0-8439-5840-5
ISBN 13: 978-0-8439-5840-9 $5.99 US/$7.99 CAN

BLOOD TRAIL TO KANSAS

ROBERT J. RANDISI

Ted Shea thinks he is a goner for sure. All the years he's worked to build his Montana spread and fine herd of prime beef means nothing if he can't sell them. And with a vicious rustler and his gang of cutthroats scaring all the hands, no one is willing to take to the trail. Until Dan Parmalee drifts into town. A gunman and gambler with a taste for long odds, he isn't about to let a little hot lead part him from some cold cash. But it doesn't take Dan long to realize this isn't just any run. This is a...*Blood Trail to Kansas*.

ISBN 10: 0-8439-5799-9
ISBN 13: 978-0-8439-5799-0 $5.99 US/$7.99 CAN

MAX BRAND®

TWISTED BARS

He was known as The Duster. Five times he'd been tried for robbery and murder, and five times acquitted. He'd met the most famous of gunmen and beaten them all. Before he gives it all up, he's got one battle left to fight. The Duster needs a proper burial for his dead partner, but the blustery Rev. Kenneth Lamont refuses to let a criminal rest in his cemetery. The Duster knows if he can't get what he wants one way, there's always another. And this is a plan the reverend won't like. Not one bit…

ISBN 10: 0-8439-5871-5
ISBN 13: 978-0-8439-5871-3 $5.99 US/$7.99 CAN

MEDICINE ROAD

WILL HENRY

Mountain man Jim Bridger is counting on Jesse Callahan. He knows that Callahan is the best man to lead the wagon train that's delivering guns and ammunition to Bridger's trading post at Green River. But Brigham Young has sworn to wipe out Bridger's posts, and he's hired Arapahoe warrior Watonga to capture those weapons at any cost. Bridger, Young and Watonga all have big plans for those guns, but it's all going to come down to just how tough Callahan can be. He's going to have to be tougher than leather if he hopes to make it to the post...alive.

ISBN 10: 0-8439-5814-6
ISBN 13: 978-0-8439-5814-0 $5.99 US/$7.99 CAN

To order a book or to request a catalog call:
1-800-481-9191
This book is also available at your local bookstore, or you can check out our Web site **www.dorchesterpub.com** where you can look up your favorite authors, read excerpts, or glance at our discussion forum to see what people have to say about your favorite books.